I

A Bad Boys of Dry River, Wyoming ~~

Book 1

Susan Fisher-Davis

Erotic Romance

Erotic Romance

Lucas
Copyright © 2015 Susan Fisher-Davis
First E-book Publication: January 2015

Cover design by Dawné Dominique
Edited by Sue Toth
Proofread by Renee Waring
All cover art copyright © 2015 by Susan Davis

ALL RIGHTS RESERVED: This literary work may not be reproduced or transmitted in any form or by any means, including electronic or photographic reproduction, in whole or in part, without express written permission.

All characters and events in this book are fictitious. Any resemblance to actual persons living or dead is strictly coincidental.

PUBLISHER
Blue Whiskey Publishing
Susan Davis
www.susanfisherdavisauthor.weebly.com

Dedication

Thank you Daniel Lerro with Dan Lerro Photography for the amazing cover shot.
Thank you Josh Phillips for that "bad boy" look. You both did an amazing job.
https://www.facebook.com/pages/Dan-Lerro-Photography

LUCAS
A Bad Boys of Dry River, Wyoming Novel
Susan Fisher-Davis
Copyright © 2015

Chapter One

Emily Walters kept her eyes trained on Lucas Taggart throughout the town meeting. She watched as he stood and left the room, drawing the eyes of most of the townspeople attending. All of the seats were full and people stood leaning against the walls. For a few more minutes, she sat there, looking toward the door he'd disappeared through before she quietly rose and followed him.

The new stop light at the intersection held no appeal for her. She'd only gone to the meeting on the chance Lucas would be there. Emily needed his help and she didn't know if she would ever get another opportunity to talk with him. According to his mother Rose, Lucas would be the perfect man for what Emily had in mind. What if he didn't come back inside and left before she had a chance to talk with him?

Not giving herself time to change her mind, she quickened her steps to catch up with him. Grabbing her coat, she practically ran out the door. The snow slapped her in the face as she ran down the concrete steps. Emily pulled her knit cap down over her ears and her coat collar up around her neck. She came to a stop and looked to the right, then to the left. Seeing him, she ran after him. The wind started howling, blowing snow around to the point she lost sight of him again.

She let out a bloodcurdling scream when he stepped from behind a pick-up truck. Her hand covered her heart. Taking a deep breath, she gazed up at him.

"I didn't mean to scare you. Sorry," he scowled.

When he reached out a hand to her, she jerked back from him. Unsettled by the look on his face, she raised her chin at him. "It's all right." He gave a terse nod and started to walk away from her. She had to act fast. "Wait! Please."

He spun around and looked at her with a tight-lipped expression. "What is it?"

Emily shivered, though she wasn't sure if it was from the cold or from this tall, brooding man. He towered over her five foot seven by at least eight inches. The snow was covering the brim and top of his black cowboy hat, the shearling coat hanging open to the cold. His dark eyes peered at her. His nose was straight and sat above a gorgeous set of lips. The scruff on his lower face and jaw only added to his good looks. His dark hair touched the collar of his coat. He raised an eyebrow at her when she didn't answer him. Sighing, he turned from her.

Emily spoke quickly. "My name is Emily Walters. Your mother told me you were back in Wyoming to settle down again. I…I need your help and I have an offer to make you."

Emily had met Lucas Taggart only once before in her life. She'd been seven at the time and he'd been a skinny boy of twelve and working on her grandfather's ranch. It was the first time she fell in love. She was in the barn every day Lucas was there. He worked there during the summer months. She'd been riding her pony when it threw her. As she laid on the ground crying, Lucas came riding by. Instead of laughing at her, he helped her up, put her on his horse, and rode her back to the ranch. She had a broken arm to show for it, but she'd fallen in love with Lucas. Her father took her down from the horse and glared at Lucas.

When Emily tried to thank Lucas, her father told her not to talk to that "bad boy." She'd looked over her father's shoulder at Lucas and saw the sad look on his face. She'd never forgotten it.

They never met again. She remembered asking her grandfather about him and he told her Lucas was always in trouble with the other boys he ran with. She never saw him again until the town meeting tonight, but she knew he'd just recently moved back to Dry River after a five-year absence.

Lucas looked at her. "Say whatever you have to say. I've got things to do."

"I want you to marry me," she said softly.

His head snapped back as if he'd been slapped. He narrowed his eyes at her.

"I'll give you half my ranch if you marry me. In name only," she continued quickly.

He didn't utter a word, just stared at her. She went on. "The ranch I'm talking about is Whispering Pines." When he hissed in a breath, she knew he was aware of the large ranch. "It's not the biggest, but it's close. The horses raised there are the best Quarter horses money can buy. They have excellent bloodlines and are in high demand." She raised her face up to him. "Well?"

He frowned and shook his head. "I know who you are now and what ranch you're talking about but I'm sure there are a number of men willing to marry you," he narrowed his eyes. "I'm not one of them."

Emily touched his arm, stopping him. "No man will marry me because they're terrified of my ex-husband, Adam Walters. He's powerful. There's not a man in Dry River who isn't afraid of him."

She raised her face to look at him. The expression on his face told her everything she needed to know. She shivered as she turned from him. No one was going to help her. Adam was going to get to her again, after all. She shook her head.

"Never mind. I'm sorry I bothered you."

Emily quickly headed back into the town hall. She should have known. No one would go up against Adam Walters. They were too afraid. She didn't know what she'd been thinking. Asking a man she'd met once, twenty years ago, to help her. Feeling the tears beginning to fall, she walked toward the rest room when she entered the town hall. Staring at herself in the mirror, she had no idea what she was going to do. She'd have to figure something else out. Lucas Taggart had been her last hope and now since he refused to help her, she was on her own.

* * * *

Lucas stared at the spot she'd been standing. He'd opened his mouth to say something, but nothing came out. He wasn't sure what he would've said anyway. Emily was a beautiful woman, but she was right. No man would marry her with Adam Walters as her ex-husband. Lucas knew who and what he was, a man who intimidated people into giving into his demands. He was in prison for extortion and embezzlement. Lucas shook his head. Walters must be getting out and it was the reason behind her wanting to get married. She wanted protection from the bastard. Lucas shook his head. What was in it for him? He grunted. Half a ranch, that's what. A very prosperous horse ranch. Something he'd always wanted. His own place. He was so tired of moving from place to place. Sighing, he silently moved back into the town hall to find Emily Walters.

He entered the room and glanced around but didn't see her anywhere. Lucas stayed at the back of the room and waited for the meeting to end. Maybe then, he'd be able to find her. The door beside him opened and Emily stepped in quietly. She glanced over to him and he could see the blush stain her cheeks. When she made a move to go to her seat, he lightly touched her arm and nodded for them to go out. She hesitated but gave a slight nod.

"Is your husband getting out of prison?" Lucas asked her as soon as they entered the lobby.

"My *ex*-husband, yes. He's being released next month. Early for good behavior." She snorted.

"That's why you're looking for a husband? To protect you?"

Emily nodded. "I'm sure he'll come looking for me."

"You think having a man around will deter him?" Lucas shook his head. "If he wants to get to you, he will. Be realistic."

"I am being realistic. He won't step foot on the ranch if he knows another man is living there."

"So, what…you're never going to leave the ranch?" He smirked. "Like I said, be realistic."

"Why did you want to talk if you weren't going to help me?"

Lucas huffed. "I didn't say I wasn't going to help. I'm thinking about it."

Emily stared up at him and waited. "What is there to think about? You'll own half of the ranch. We'll be in a partnership."

"*What is there to think about?* Are you serious? You're talking marriage here. I'm not looking to get married and if I do, I want it to be for life. I'd want to have children." Lucas sighed. "If you want to do this, then it has to be a real marriage."

Emily gasped. "We don't know each other."

"We've known each other for years, just not closely. We'd take our time getting to know each other better before we'd make it real. If I'm going to have a wife, she's going to be a real wife," He stared at her. "That's the deal. Take it or leave it," He spun away from her and started walking away when her words stopped him.

"I'll take it," she whispered.

Lucas spun around to face her. "What?"

She cleared her throat. "I said...I'll take it."

Lucas stared at her then nodded. "How soon do you need to do this?"

"As I said, he's being released next month so as soon as possible."

"And I get half of the ranch?" Lucas needed clarification.

"Yes. I'll have my attorney draw up the papers."

"Your grandfather left you the ranch?"

"Yes. I was all he had at the end. My dad passed away two years before grandpa did. I never knew my mother," Emily told him.

Lucas's jaw tightened. "Yes. I remember your father."

"I'm sorry he treated you the way he did," Emily said softly.

Lucas grunted. "He wasn't the only one."

Lucas was one of the "bad boys" of Dry River. Along with five others, they tore up the town from the time they were twelve. They'd been inseparable and even though they all didn't reside in Wyoming, they were still close. They were the boys mothers warned their daughters about and fathers had nightmares about but the older they got, the more the women wanted them. There wasn't a single woman in town who didn't want a chance with them. Some married ones too. Now here he was contemplating marriage with a woman he'd known for years but didn't really know at all. His gaze roamed over her face. She was beautiful. A knit cap covered her dark hair, only her bangs showed. Her eyes were jade green with thick lush lashes, a pert nose sitting above a Cupid's bow mouth. *Shit!* It wouldn't be a hardship to go to bed with her but...*marriage.* Lucas ran his hand down his face.

"Let me know when you get with the attorney. I want it specified if we happen to divorce for whatever reason I still retain part ownership of the ranch." He knew by the look on her face the thought hadn't entered her mind. "Is that a problem?"

"No. I'll call you in few days. Are you staying with your mother?"

"No. She recently remarried and I don't want to be a bother. I'll be at Cooper's. You can call me there." He spun on his heel and walked away from her.

* * * *

Emily watched as Lucas strode out the door as if the hounds of hell were chasing him. Not a real confidence booster. She sighed and smiled. He was going to do it. He was going to marry her. The smile left her face as she thought about a real marriage with him. She'd have to sleep with him. Shivering, she rubbed her hands up and down her arms. Was he serious about wanting to stay married? Emily was only thinking short-term but a lasting marriage may not be so bad. As long as Lucas treated her well, maybe they could make it work. She sighed and moved out the doors to head for home.

When she pulled through the stone pillars, she felt a sense of pride. Her grandfather ran the ranch with an iron fist and it prospered because of it. The men loved and hated him, but there was always respect. When he died, the ranch hands grieved right alongside her. Now, she ran the ranch, and none of the men had a problem with it. They had watched her grow up. They were well aware she knew every inch of Whispering Pines. She'd only left it when she'd married Adam and she returned to her roots once he was in prison. While he was there, she divorced him.

Pulling up to the large white farmhouse, she stopped by the back door. The wind was whipping around, blowing the snow sideways. Taking a deep breath, Emily pushed the door open and the snow hit her in the face. Gasping, she hopped out, ran up the steps, and entered through the back door and into the kitchen. She sighed with relief at the warmth of the house. The house, though built in the eighteen hundreds, had a modern feel about it with the cherry cabinets, black granite counter tops, and black appliances. Her Maine Coon cat, Munchkin, meowed at her.

"Give me a minute, Munch. I just came in the door. I'm sure your dinner can wait." Emily laughed when the cat gave her a look of disdain and strolled over to her dish and gazed up at her. "Let me get my coat off. Is that too much to ask?"

Munchkin sat on the huge braid rug that covered cherry hardwood floors and proceeded to lick her paws as if she couldn't be bothered, but she came to attention when she heard the can opener running. She weaved in and out of Emily's legs, almost tripping her a few times. Emily dumped the food into the dish and Munchkin ate it with gusto.

"Munch, we're going to have a man in the house." Emily stopped when the cat glared up at her. "I know. I'm sorry but I need him here." She squatted down to pet the cat. "We need to have him here in case Adam comes here." At Adam's name, Munch growled. Emily laughed. "I know. You hate him as much as I do."

Emily stood and walked through the hallway toward the front foyer. To her left was a large formal dining room and to her right was the living room with a fireplace taking up the center wall. Two large windows ran alongside it. The foyer was open with gleaming hardwood floors. The stairs ran along the wall of the dining room. She headed upstairs to relax in the tub. The large claw foot tub seemed to be calling her name. She poured bubble bath under the running faucet and undressed as the tub filled up. After piling her long hair on top of her head, she lowered herself into the tub, sighing. The moon's beams glimmered through the large window, above the tub. She leaned her head back and closed her eyes then jerked them open when Munch jumped up onto the side of the tub.

"Hey pretty girl. Is your belly full now?" Emily smiled when Munch butted her head against hers. "I hope I'm doing the right thing here, Munch. Lucas was my first crush. I was in love as much as a seven-year-old girl can be." Emily laughed when she heard Munch purring. "I hope you like him. I know you hated Adam but Lucas isn't anything like him." She nibbled on her bottom lip. "At least, I don't think he is. His mother is nice. I'm glad I got to know her, otherwise I wouldn't have been able to talk to her and have her help me." Munch meowed and jumped down. Emily watched as she left the room, tail high in the air. Emily sighed and stepped from the tub. After wrapping the navy blue towel around her, she moved toward her bedroom and sat on her bed. Munch was already on the bed in her usual spot.

"Am I making a mistake, Munch? How am I going to marry a man I don't really know or love? Will it really keep Adam away if he sees me as a married woman?" She chuckled when Munch growled at the mention of Adam again. "He was awful to you, wasn't he, precious girl?"

Munch blinked her big eyes at Emily, yawned, and closed her eyes. She was done with the conversation. So was Emily. Tomorrow she'd contact her attorney and then call Lucas so they could set a date to get married. She blew out a breath, knowing she had no other options.

* * * *

"Are you out of your mind?" Cooper Lang stared at him.

"No. She needs help and I'm going to get half her ranch for helping her," Lucas told his friend.

"But…*marriage?* You *are* out of your mind."

"It's time I settled down anyway. We're thirty-two now. Shouldn't we have a wife and kids by now?"

Cooper stared at him and then burst out laughing. "Hell no. Come on Lucas. You can't be serious. You don't even know her for God's sake. What the hell are you thinking?"

Lucas pulled out a chair and took a seat at the table. "I'm thinking it's going to be my only chance to have my own place." He glanced at Cooper. "You know it's what I want. Whispering Pines is a gorgeous spread."

Cooper sobered. "I know it is but damn, Lucas. Are you sure you want to marry Emily just for half a ranch? You have enough money to buy your own place."

"I've done nothing but think about it for days and…yes, I do for the chance to have a place to call my own. A place already up and running. Now, are you going to be my best man or not?"

"You know I will but I still think you're making a big mistake."

"I guess we'll see, won't we? You need to settle down too."

"Oh hell no. Not me, man."

Lucas laughed. "You might meet that one special woman one day and not have a choice."

"Well, she better be pretty damn special to get me to the altar," Cooper laughed.

Lucas shook his head. The two men talked for a while then headed outside to the barn. Although Cooper ran a successful motorcycle design shop, he still ran a cattle ranch. With his father gone, he kept the ranch running. If he had a bike to work on, his ranch hands were more than capable of running the ranch.

Later, as they sat in the living room watching TV, Lucas couldn't stop thinking of Emily. He remembered her as a little girl who fell off her pony. Her big green eyes filled with tears as he helped her up and put her on his horse so he could take her back to the ranch. It was just lucky for her he'd been out looking for one of the horses which hadn't returned to the barn. Her father, however, hadn't been nice at all. He never said thank you for bringing her home. Lucas knew Emily felt bad about it. She in no way resembled a little girl anymore. Now she was a gorgeous woman. She was tall, but still only came to his chin. He wanted to see her dark hair. Did she wear it short or long? Shaking his head, he stood and walked toward the kitchen for a beer. The phone rang and he yelled to Cooper he'd get it.

"Lang residence."

"Could I speak to Lucas, please?" a soft feminine voice asked.

"This is Lucas. Emily, is that you?"

"Yes. The lawyer has the papers drawn up. All you have to do is sign them. We could get...," she cleared her throat. "we could get married the day you sign them. If you haven't changed your mind."

"I haven't. What day do you want to do this? I've asked Cooper to be my best man."

"Is Wednesday of next week all right with you? That's the day my attorney wants you to go into his office and sign the papers. So we can meet there at ten and then go to the courthouse."

"That's fine. I'll see you there." Lucas listened as she told him the address of the attorney then hung up. He turned to see Cooper leaning against the doorjamb with his arms folded across his broad chest.

"So you're really going to do this?" Cooper shook his head. "I was hoping since you hadn't heard from her, she'd changed her mind."

"I'm doing this. If you don't want to be a part of it, that's fine. I can get one of the other guys to do it." Lucas glared at his friend.

"I said I'd do it, for Christ's sake, even though I think you're making one hell of a mistake. Not just for marrying her but because of her crazy ass husband. He could kill you. He's nuts."

"I know, but I don't think he wants to risk going back to prison."

"Doesn't mean he won't have someone do it for him. I know he treated Emily like shit. It was all over town."

"Did he hit her?" Lucas's temperature started rising.

"No. He verbally abused her. Called her names, told her she was stupid. Verbal's as bad as physical in my book," Cooper said.

"Son of a bitch. I'd like to see him on the ranch so I can kick his ass."

"We're doing this when?" Cooper sighed.

Lucas told him everything he had to do and they agreed to meet at the courthouse next Wednesday at eleven. Cooper nodded then left the room. Lucas blew out a breath. He was really going to do this.

* * * *

Two days later, Lucas pulled onto the road to Cooper's house and was surprised to see several trucks parked close to the house. It wouldn't have caught his attention if they were close to the barn where the motorcycle shop sat. Shaking his head, he walked inside and came to a halt when he saw three of his closest friends sitting around the table. They all glanced up at him when he entered. He flattened his lips.

"What the fuck is this? An intervention?" Lucas asked as he slipped his coat and hat off and hung them up.

"Something like that," Cooper told him. "I called the guys to tell them you were getting married." He shrugged. "They came over."

Lucas took in each of his friend's stares. Lincoln Cole and Storm Bateman. The only ones missing were Montgomery Bradford and Dakota Walker and Lucas knew they'd be there if they didn't live out of town.

Lucas glanced over to Cooper. "I'm doing this." He glanced around the table. "None of you are going to change my mind."

"Why are you even considering this, Lucas?" Lincoln asked. "You have more than enough money to start your own ranch."

"As I told Cooper, Whispering Pines is already up and running. It would take me years to get a place of my own to such a status." Lucas took a seat beside Lincoln.

"But to get married? Why can't you just stay there with her until her ex leaves her alone? Hell, you don't even know if he'll show up," Lincoln said.

"She thinks he will and she wants him to know she's remarried and…happy. In love with her new husband. That she's moved on and he should too. Emily is afraid of him and I'll keep her safe." Lucas narrowed his eyes at them. "I'm doing this. With or without your blessing. You're my friends and I expect you to support me." He glanced around the table. "All of you."

All of the men started muttering. Cooper stood. "He's right. We need to support him no matter what his decision." Cooper sighed. "We don't have to agree with him, we just need to support him."

Lucas nodded. "I'm doing it no matter what you all think." He stood. "I don't need your approval." He strode from the room and headed to his bedroom, slamming the door behind him. Damn them. They were his friends. His best friends and they should be there for him. It's all he asked, that they be there. He was taking a big step. Emily too. She couldn't be any more comfortable about this than he was. It wasn't going to be easy being married to a woman he barely knew. What he said about getting a ranch up and running was true and he'd always dreamed of owning a place like Whispering Pines. Working there as a boy, he'd fallen in love with the place. He dreamed every night of owning a horse ranch like it. To have part ownership in it was amazing. Buying a ranch now would take years to get it to prosper. He'd be an old man by then. Lucas wanted a ranch he could enjoy now. He wanted to be able to work with the horses since he loved them so much. Hands on is what he wanted and needed. He'd have it now if he married Emily. He shook his head. There was no *if* about it. They were getting married and that was final. If his friends couldn't accept it, so be it.

Chapter Two

Wednesday morning was sunny and blustery cold. The weatherman announced more snow was expected. Emily put her coat on and trudged outside to warm up her SUV. The cold was like a slap in the face when she stepped out onto the porch. After starting the vehicle, she ran back inside. Munch sat in the center of the kitchen staring up at her.

"Stay out of the other bedroom. I made it up for Lucas, not you. I'll be back later and introduce you to him. You'd better be nice." Emily stared at the cat. When Munch started licking her paws, Emily knew she'd been dismissed.

A knock on the door made her let out a startled cry. She spun around and saw Tinker, the foreman, standing on the porch. She opened the door and motioned for him to come in. He took his cowboy hat off, stared at her, and finally sighed.

"Are you sure you want to do this?" Tinker asked. She'd told him soon after Lucas agreed to marry her and Tinker wasn't happy about it. "I can take of things on the ranch."

"It's not that, Tinker, and you know it. You, of all people, should know how ruthless Adam is. He's not afraid of you," Emily told the man who'd been like a father to her since she was born. Tinker Andrews was sixty-seven years old. He'd been on the ranch since he was eighteen and fresh out of school. Emily had grown up right before his eyes. He'd watched her learn to ride a horse, fall in love, get her heart broken, and fall in love again, with the wrong man, and he saw her come home a broken woman due to the abuse of her husband. She knew Tinker was never happier than when she'd divorced Adam.

"I know, but Lucas Taggart? He's rough around the edges. I don't want to see you hurt again." Tinker stared at her.

"Please don't worry about me. I'm a big girl now and I know better than to let a man treat me like that again. Lucas is not a bad man. He was wild when he was younger but I'm sure he's grown out of it. He's going to help out around here, he's good with horses, and he'll protect me. Something you can't do, Tinker. You have enough to do around here without worrying about me. I don't want you to get involved if Adam does show up." She put her hands on her hips and narrowed her eyes at him. "That's an order."

Tinker smirked. "Yes ma'am."

Emily grinned. "Thank you. I have to go. I'm picking Kendra up on the way." She kissed his cheek. "Thank you for wanting to take care of me but I'll be fine and I'll feel much better with Lucas in the house."

Tinker nodded then left. Emily sighed. This was it. She was getting married. Her ivory dress consisted of lace and pearl buttons. The dress stopped just above her ankles. On her feet were snow boots but she was changing once she got into town into a pair of white stilettos. She smiled, wondering what Lucas would think if she wore the boots to their wedding. Shrugging, she put her coat on and got into her SUV. Taking a deep breath, she pulled out of the driveway and drove toward town to get married.

She pulled up to Kendra's house and blew the horn. Kendra Mattingly came running out the door and hopped into the vehicle. She smiled at Emily.

"You're really doing this, huh?"

Emily sighed. "Everyone keeps asking me that. Yes. I'm doing this. You know how Adam treated me and with him getting out, I don't want him coming around. I know he'll come to Whispering Pines to look for me. If only to let me know he's here, but he will show up. I've thought about it and he'll want revenge for divorcing him while he was in prison." She shook her head. "I know he hates that I divorced him. I could've never done it if he weren't in prison. He'd never let me go."

Kendra nodded. "That's true. He was obsessed with you. I'm so afraid what's going to happen if he shows up."

"When. When he shows up. The more I think about it the more I know he'll come looking for me. It's why I want to go through with this. At first, I wasn't sure Adam would show. He will, but I won't be alone. Lucas is a big man and he won't bow down to Adam like other men will. I'm not sure the ranch hands would even stand up to him to protect me."

"I know and that's why I'm scared but I do think I'll feel better knowing Lucas is there." Kendra glanced at her. "He sure is hot, isn't he?"

Emily shrugged. "I haven't noticed."

Kendra burst out laughing. "You never were a very good liar, Em."

Emily glanced at her friend and sighed. "He is, isn't he?"

"Yes. He's a gorgeous sexy man. I remember him and his friends running around town getting into trouble all the time, but the older they got the more the girls were chasing them. All of them were gorgeous. I saw him at the town meeting and was shocked at just how gorgeous he was."

"I didn't get to see much of them when I was growing up. I was always at the ranch helping out but I always heard about their escapades." Emily shook her head. "My dad didn't like any of them. Maybe it's why he kept me on the ranch." She laughed.

They pulled into the parking lot of the attorney's office and headed inside. Emily stumbled a little when she saw Lucas and Cooper standing in the lobby. Both of them were dressed in western cut suits and looking handsome. Her eyes roamed over Lucas's tall body and she shivered. His eyes met hers as she glided toward him and stopped in front of him.

"You ready to do this?" he asked in a low voice.

"Yes. Are you?" She tilted her head and watched as his lips curved into a smile.

"I am."

All of them sat and waited. Emily noticed Kendra and Cooper didn't speak. What was that about? The door to the office opened and Maxwell Barr stepped out and told her and Lucas to enter his office. They followed him inside and took a seat. He shuffled papers around then glared at Lucas before looking at Emily.

"It's not too late to change your mind, Emily."

She heard Lucas grunt. "I'm not changing my mind, Max. Let's get these papers signed."

Max nodded at her and shoved the paper toward her and showed her where to sign then moved it to Lucas and showed him. He seemed to hesitate. Emily glanced over to him and watched him take a deep breath.

"Maybe it isn't you I should be saying it's not too late to, Emily." Max smirked.

Lucas picked up the pen and signed his name. Emily sighed with relief. They stood and left the office. Emily was surprised to see Cooper and Kendra on opposite sides of the waiting room. She frowned at Kendra when she glanced up from a magazine. Kendra shrugged and stood. Lucas didn't seem to notice anything amiss.

The four of them walked to their vehicles and drove to the courthouse. Emily parked beside Lucas's truck and turned in her seat to reach for her stilettos. All her hand grasped was air. She spun in the seat and searched.

"Oh no. Please no."

"What is it?" Kendra turned to her.

Emily looked at her friend. "I left my shoes at the house."

Kendra snickered. "You're kidding right?"

Emily glared at her. "Does it look like I'm kidding? Now I have to get married in snow boots." She glanced down at Kendra's feet.

Kendra shook her head. "We don't wear the same size. Your size six will not go into my size five."

Emily growled. "I can't believe I did that. I jinxed it when I wondered what Lucas would think if I showed up in snow boots."

"You had a lot on your mind I'm sure. You'll just have to get married in your boots or barefoot."

Emily groaned. "Let's do this."

They entered the courthouse to see Lucas and Cooper already there. Lucas walked towards her and stopped in his tracks when he glanced down to her feet and smiled.

"Not one word, Lucas. I forgot my shoes." Emily glared up at him.

He raised his hands in mock surrender. "I wasn't going to say anything."

Emily removed her coat and heard him hiss in a breath. She quickly glanced up at him. "What is it? Do I have something on my dress?" She quickly looked down at her dress.

"No. You look...beautiful," Lucas whispered.

Emily could feel the heat in her cheeks. "Thank you. You look very handsome in your suit."

Lucas grumbled. "Don't get used to it. I hate wearing these things."

Emily laughed. "All right." She took a deep breath. "You ready?"

"As I'll ever be. Let's go." He put his hand out to her. After a slight hesitation, she placed her hand in his and felt a jolt. She glanced up at him but he didn't seem to feel anything. Mentally shrugging, she let him lead her into the judge's chambers.

They recited their vows and when it came time to exchange rings, Emily almost panicked. She'd forgotten about the rings. She watched as Lucas reached inside his jacket, pulled out two plain gold bands, and handed one to Kendra to hold. Emily smiled up at him and then nervously waited for the kiss. Lucas kissed her quickly as if he didn't want to at all. They left the courthouse after getting their license and met back at the ranch. It seemed ridiculous to Emily for a man and woman just married to travel in separate cars but she had to take Kendra home. Cooper had driven his own vehicle.

* * * *

Lucas drove to the ranch to wait for Emily. He sat in the truck and looked around. American Quarter Horses filled the two red barns, some of the most sought after in the United States. A championship bloodline ran through them. The demand for them was high. Lucas couldn't wait to work with them. He loved horses and to work with these was a dream come true. Not only that, he had ownership in them. His gaze swept over to the Big Horn Mountains in the distance. The snow moving in from the mountains covered the tips. Lucas knew it would be in Dry River later in the day. His gaze moved back to the house. He'd always been in awe of the large farmhouse with the wraparound porch. When he first started working at Whispering Pines, he would make believe he lived there. Emily would run around the porch, giggling, while her grandfather would chase her. Lucas would watch, envying them and secretly want to join in the fun but he never did. His mother did a good job of raising him until he turned twelve, then he thought he knew everything. He and his friends tore up the town. The older they got, the more trouble they'd gotten into. They'd even spent a night or two in the local jail.

He glanced in the rearview mirror when he saw Emily pulling in behind him. She was so beautiful. Her dark hair was up in some sort of bun and he was anxious to see it down, spread across a pillow. He grunted. That sure wasn't going to happen very soon. They had to get to know each other first. The kiss after the ceremony about threw him to his knees and it had only been a little peck. She'd looked so beautiful in her gown. Even with the snow boots on her feet. Lucas closed his eyes and groaned. This was going to be harder than he thought.

Sighing, he opened his door, stepped out, and waited for her to reach him. He reached into the bed of the truck to get his duffle bag. She smiled up at him shyly and then led him into the house. The biggest cat he'd ever seen sat in the center of the kitchen glaring at him. He glanced at Emily.

"Why do you need me here when you have that cat? He looks like he could take down anyone."

"*She*. Munch doesn't much care for men."

"Great." Lucas muttered. "Munch? What kind of name is Munch?"

"It's short for Munchkin. She'll tolerate you, just like she does me, but cross her and she'll make your life miserable." Emily smiled.

"I have no desire to get close enough to cross her. I'm not a cat person."

"Get used to her. She's not going anywhere," Emily said angrily.

"I didn't say she was. Don't get so testy."

Emily sighed. "I'm sorry. Adam hated her."

"Did she just growl at me?" Lucas raised his eyebrows.

Emily burst out laughing. "No. She growled because I said Adam. She hated him right back." Munch growled again.

Lucas shook his head. "Amazing. I hope she doesn't have a problem with me. I don't want to wake up one night with her sitting on my chest plotting my death."

Emily chuckled. "Would you like some coffee?"

Lucas shook his head. "No thanks. I just want to get out of this monkey suit and relax a little. I didn't sleep much last night."

She nodded. "I didn't either. Come with me, I'll show you to your room."

Lucas picked up the duffle bag and followed her upstairs. She entered a large bedroom.

"If this room isn't to your liking. You can choose from four others. I gave you this one since it has a bathroom. The bathroom is between our rooms." He saw her cheeks flush and held back a smile. "I thought you'd want to have a bathroom. There are two full baths up here and a half bath downstairs. For such a large home, it should have more." She shrugged. "Anyway, if you stay in this room, please lock my door to the bathroom when you're in it and I'll do the same. I'm sure we don't want to surprise each other in the shower."

"Why not?" Lucas asked softly.

Her head snapped up. "What?"

Lucas smiled. "Relax. I was joking."

She let out a breath. "Oh. Um...okay, I'll let you unpack and get some rest. I'm going to do the same. I'll introduce you to everyone later."

Lucas nodded. He'd love to rest with her but he'd take his time. She was his wife and eventually she would be in every sense of the word. He felt his groin tighten at the thought. *Son of a bitch!* It couldn't be soon enough. His gaze swept around the room and took in the antique furnishings. The dark walnut headboard almost touched the ceiling. An old dresser with a mirror held up by spindles sat in a corner. A row of windows allowed him to gaze down into the yard. He sighed as he tossed his duffle bag on the bed. After he undressed, he laid down and fell asleep.

* * * *

Later in the afternoon, Emily woke up and walked downstairs. She heard voices coming from the kitchen. She stopped in the doorway and watched as Tinker and Lucas stood glaring at each other.

"What's going on?" Emily asked. Both men jumped and looked her way.

Tinker cleared his throat. "We were, uh...just talking."

"Yes. It looked like quite an animated conversation."

Lucas turned from her. Tinker stared at the floor.

"You two have to get along." Emily waited for Tinker to look at her. "He's your boss, Tinker. Just as I am."

"Yes, ma'am," Tinker mumbled.

"I just want to work alongside the men. I don't want to step on anyone's toes. Tinker runs the place. I'm not overstepping that." Lucas glanced at Tinker. "I trust your judgment. If Emily does, then it's good enough for me."

Tinker nodded. "Good enough." He stuck his hand out and Lucas shook it.

Emily sighed. "Good. Now, Tinker can you take Lucas out to meet the men?"

"Sure." He jerked his chin for Lucas to head out the door.

"Tinker." Emily said as soon as Lucas stepped outside. Tinker turned toward her. "Do you want to tell me what that was about?"

Tinker's ears turned red. "I told him if he hurt you, I'd be all over him."

Emily bit her lip to keep from smiling. Lucas stood six three, Tinker barely reached five nine and skinny where Lucas had a big body. He looked like nothing but solid muscle. The idea of Tinker trying to take him on was laughable, but she appreciated it.

"Thank you, but I think we'll be fine." Emily hugged him and squeezed tighter when Tinker wrapped his arms around her.

"I might not be able to take him on physically but I have a rifle." He spun around and left. Emily stared after him. She shook her head as she walked to the door and peered out the window. Lucas was already at the barn with Tinker lagging behind.

She sighed and headed to the office to do some paperwork. What a way to spend your wedding day.

* * * *

Lucas waited for Tinker to enter the barn behind him. When he did, the older man glared at him. Lucas sighed.

"Look Tinker, we have to live on this ranch together and it's not going to be possible with all the hostility you're throwing at me. Emily and I are married and I own half this ranch. We need to, at least, be civil to each other."

"I don't want that girl hurt. I saw her heart get broken before and I won't watch her go through it again." Tinker put his hands on his hips and glared up at Lucas. The ranch hands in the barn stopped working to watch the exchange.

"First off, Emily isn't a girl anymore. She's a grown woman and old enough to make her own decisions. Secondly, I'm her *husband* and I expect respect from all of you. I really don't give a shit what you say about me behind my back but to my face you will be respectful. Is that clear?" Lucas moved his eyes to each man and nodded when they all gave him a nod. His gaze returned to Tinker. "Now show me around. I'm anxious to work with these beauties."

Tinker hesitated then showed Lucas where he could start. Lucas gave a terse nod and went to work. He knew how to do everything needed to keep a horse healthy, from filing teeth to inoculations. After working at several large ranches, he'd learned everything he could. He'd grown up in the little town of Dry River, but he'd needed to get out for some reason or other. He'd been restless and the itch to move kept at him like a spot he couldn't reach to scratch. Lucas hoped the drifting was over and done. The thought of having his own place was always in the back of his mind. Every time he worked at someone else's place, he felt he was wasting his life away.

As he took a shoe off one of the horses, he felt a little pride he finally had a place. He had more than enough money put back to buy his own place but Whispering Pines was the place to be. Lucas knew it in his bones. He just didn't expect to be married this way. His wife slept in one room and he slept in another. Shaking his head, he went back to work. The day passed quickly. Before long, it was time to quit for the day. The ranch hands came over to him and introduced themselves.

"Yeah, I'm sorry we didn't get to it earlier," Lucas muttered.

"That's all right boss," one of the younger hands said.

Lucas shook his head. "I'm not your boss. Tinker is. Don't ever forget it."

The hands all nodded and left. Lucas turned to leave and saw Tinker staring at him. Lucas hung his head and put his hands on his hips. Blowing out a breath, he raised his head to look at Tinker.

"What is it now?"

Tinker strode toward him. "I heard what you just told the men. I appreciate it."

"It's the truth, Tinker. You're their boss. I just happen to be yours." Lucas shrugged and grinned.

Tinker's eyes widened then he burst out laughing. "Yes you are." He stuck his hand out. "Let's do this again. Welcome to Whispering Pines, Mr. Taggart."

Lucas shook his hand. "Call me Lucas."

Tinker nodded. They grinned at each other and left the barn together. Tinker moved on to the bunkhouse he lived in on the property, and Lucas headed for the house. Walking in the back door, he came to a halt when he saw Emily bent over peering into the refrigerator. Her jeans stretched across her ass. He swallowed hard.

She straightened up and spun around. When she saw him standing there she placed her hands on her hips and glared at him. Lucas raised his eyes to her face. He was trying not to smile.

"What?" he asked innocently.

"Are you serious?"

Lucas chuckled. "I'm not apologizing. Can't a man look at his wife's, uh…attributes?"

* * * *

Emily couldn't think. His grin was gorgeous. His teeth were white, straight, and perfect. The dimples in his cheeks deepened and his chuckle sent a shiver along her spine. The man was drop dead gorgeous.

"I…" she shook her head. "I have no answer for that."

Lucas laughed. "I've got you speechless?"

Did he ever. And it had nothing to do with his comment. Those dark eyes were gorgeous. She wondered if she had drool dripping from her mouth. Her husband was one hot man. She could feel the heat in her cheeks as she gazed up at him. The smile left his face as their eyes met and held. When his gaze dropped to her lips, she couldn't help but lick them.

She watched as Lucas closed his eyes as if in pain. When he opened them, he took a step toward her. A knock on the back door caused him to halt in his tracks. He spun around and opened the door. Tinker stood there. His gaze going back and forth between them.

"Did you need something, Tinker?" Emily asked.

"I'm going to make a run to the feed store tomorrow. We're low on oats and I want to make sure we have plenty. There's a big storm coming, but I'll get back before it starts in the morning."

"That's fine, Tinker. Go get what you need," Emily told him. He narrowed his eyes at Lucas then glanced at her. She smiled. Tinker nodded and left.

"That's some babysitter you have there," Lucas told her as he took his coat off.

"Tinker's known me since I was in diapers. He's like a father to me. He doesn't want to see me hurt."

"I get it. You have six men besides him working here, why do you need me?"

Emily huffed. "I need a man in the house and before you say anything, having a ranch hand in here wouldn't keep Adam away. He'd just figure he could pay him off. If Adam thinks I'm...in love with my husband and he loves me, he won't come near the house."

"What about when you're in town?"

"He won't bother me with other people around. Dry River has eyes everywhere. I'll be safe in town and here. Those are the only places I go. I work here and run to town only when I need to." Emily shrugged. "He'll know I'm married. He's kept tabs on me. I also had a private detective keeping them on him."

"He may not even show up."

Emily laughed. "He will, if only to let me know he's around so he can torment me. As soon as I heard he was being released I got a restraining order against him but it won't stop him."

"Do you think he'll try to do you physical harm?"

"I don't know." She shook her head. "I really don't know."

"He'll have to go through me," Lucas said softly.

Emily smiled up at him. "Thank you."

He smiled. "Isn't that what husbands do? Protect their family?"

"Yes."

Lucas stepped toward her, stopping in front of her. He slowly raised his hands and cupped her face. She looked into his eyes.

"I'm going to kiss my wife," Lucas whispered as he lowered his head. His lips brushed hers lightly. When she moaned, he ran his tongue along the seam of her lips. "Open for me." His lips tickled hers as he spoke. Her mouth opened and his tongue moved inside to the deep honeyed depths.

Emily's hands moved up his chest to around his neck. Her fingers splayed through his hair. Lucas groaned into her mouth and moved his hands down her neck to her shoulders and around her back. He cupped her butt and pulled her tightly against him. She could feel his erection pressing against her stomach and slowly pulled back from him. Lucas stepped back.

"You're not going to hit me, are you?" He raised an eyebrow at her.

Emily laughed. "No. It was both our faults."

"I wouldn't call it a fault of any kind." Lucas shrugged. "I'd say we both enjoyed it."

Emily nodded. "Yes. I agree." She smiled shyly at him and glanced away.

"So…you want to go to bed?"

Emily's head whipped around. She narrowed her eyes when she saw him grinning. Her mouth twitched. "That isn't funny."

"I don't think it is either." He strode past her then stopped at the doorway of the kitchen. "If you change your mind, you know where to find me."

Emily watched him walk away. She could hear him going up the stairs and into the bathroom. When the shower started, she groaned as she pictured him in there. His big body getting wet from the water sluicing down over him. Emily pulled out a chair, sat down, and put her hands over her face. How was she going to do this, not sleep with the man she married. She slapped her hands down on the table. That wasn't right. They would eventually sleep together. She snorted. Sleep had nothing to do with it.

Chapter Three

The day of his release, Adam strode through the gate and stopped. He took a deep breath of fresh air. Freedom had never tasted so sweet. Revenge was going to taste even sweeter. His ride sat across the street waiting for him. He crossed over, got into the passenger seat, and smiled at the woman behind the wheel. Stella Carlisle was beautiful, but dumber than shit, as far as he was concerned. She didn't realize he'd used her. They started out as pen pals but once she visited him in prison, she fell in love. Adam almost laughed. She actually believed he loved her too, and since she did, she'd do anything he asked of her. Including driving him to Dry River to see his ex-wife. He snorted and she glanced over at him.

"What was that for, honey?" she cooed.

"Just thinking of being out of the hell hole and how great it feels. Let's get going. I want to talk to Emily as soon as possible."

Stella stuck her bottom lip out. "Do you have to see her? Can't you just call her?"

Adam curbed his anger. "I told you, she has an unlisted number now and I need to talk to her about the ranch." He put his hand on her nape. "You know the ranch you and I are going to live on once she signs over her share."

Adam had told Stella he owned half of Whispering Pines, when in reality he owned none of it. He'd told her Emily agreed to sign over her half and he would live there with Stella. *Stupid bitch!* He just needed a ride to Dry River and he'd get rid of Stella once he got there. She was a loose end. One of many. The anger he felt over hearing Emily was married again was tangible. He couldn't wait to get there and kill her and her husband. Adam became a bitter man in prison and he'd never go back for any reason. He had plans to head north after killing them and Stella. All he had to do was get there, check out the setup of the ranch, and carry out his plan. He grinned. The time couldn't come soon enough.

Lucas saw Emily jump when he came through the back door. He raised an eyebrow at her.

"Relax," he said softly.

She nodded. "I'm trying. He was released today."

Lucas chuckled. "I know. You've told me several times today."

"I'm sorry." She turned away from him and rubbed her arms.

Lucas moved to stand behind her and placed his hands on her shoulders. He turned her to face him. "We'll be fine. The men will keep an eye out and I'm not stepping off the ranch without you."

Emily wrapped her arms around his waist and nodded. "I know. I'm just scared. I know he's going to come here." She gazed up at Lucas.

"I'll be ready for him." He lowered his head and pressed his lips to hers. His hands slid down her back to her hips. He pulled her tight against him and deepened the kiss. Lucas wanted her with a passion he didn't even know he possessed.

Emily pulled back from him and smiled shyly up at him. "I hope we're all ready for him."

Lucas gazed down into her face. "We all know to be on the lookout for him. If he shows up."

"He will show up, Lucas. I have no doubt in my mind." Emily moved around him and took a seat at the table.

Lucas sat down next to her and took her hands in his. "We're ready for him, Emily."

Emily shook her head. "He's so devious. He could hire people to come here."

"We know everyone in this town so if a stranger shows up we're prepared to take them on." Lucas sighed. "I know you're scared but we're all going to be watching for him or any strangers in town. The men here know to keep an eye out and I've informed my friends to watch, too. Adam is known here. I'm sure if he shows up himself, people will be talking."

Emily nodded. "Yes, I'm sure you're right."

"I need to get back out to the barn." He abruptly stood and left.

* * * *

Emily stared at the spot he'd been sitting. She hoped he was right. Lucas had no idea how evil Adam could be. Although he'd never physically hurt her, he was sadistic in his treatment of her. He swore he'd never let her go. Ever. Once she divorced him in prison, he probably began plotting what he'd do to her once he was released. She was terrified of him coming after her. When she filed for divorce, he tried to fight it but her attorney had no problem showing grounds for divorce, with him being in prison the main reason for her divorcing him.

Emily sighed and headed back to the office to work on the books. Owning one of the best Quarter horse ranches kept her busy. Since it was Thursday, she needed to get payroll ready for tomorrow. She glanced out the window and groaned when she saw the snow coming down heavily. Great. She was so ready for winter to be over but being in northern Wyoming, it could linger quite a while.

An hour later, Emily stood and stretched. The payroll was finished. All the men received their checks by direct deposit but they still received copies of their checks. Emily put her coat on and headed out the door to give the men their paystubs.

The crisp cold air took her breath away. The blowing snow made it almost impossible to see. She pulled her knit cap down over her ears and the collar of her jacket up around her chin. The Wyoming winters were the only thing she didn't care for but it was something she'd learned to live with. As a child, she'd loved the snow, but as she got older, she realized what a burden it was. The horses stayed near the barns when it was snowing this badly. It was too easy to lose them in the pastures during a blizzard. Emily trudged through the snow to the barn. When she stepped inside, she waited until her eyes adjusted before she moved any further. She glanced around and didn't see any of the men. Frowning, she moved toward the back office and heard their voices. She opened the door and they all turned to stare at her.

"Why are you all in here? Isn't there work to be done?"

They seemed embarrassed to be caught sitting around. Lucas stood and moved toward her. "We were just getting warmed up before we headed back out. Is that all right…boss?"

Emily gazed up at him. "Sure…boss. It's fine." She smiled up at him.

His eyes met hers and held until Tinker cleared his throat. Emily felt her cheeks warming up. She nodded at Lucas.

"I'll, uh…just go back to the house." She handed him the envelopes. "Please hand these out." She practically ran out the door.

When she stepped inside the house, she took her cap and coat off, then took a seat at the table. Putting her hands over her face, she groaned. It was getting harder and harder to be around Lucas and not want him. She jerked when the back door opened and he strolled in and walked toward her then stopped in front of her. He took his cowboy hat off and tossed it onto the table. She stared up at him.

"Stand up," Lucas ordered.

Emily didn't question him, she stood and faced him. His eyes raked over her face and stopped at her lips. Lucas groaned and pulled her toward him.

"I need this," he whispered right before his lips took hers in a deep kiss. Emily's arms circled around his neck. Her fingers plowed through his thick hair. She was surprised when he quickly ended the kiss, picked up his hat and strode out the door.

* * * *

Lucas strode outside to cool off. This was damn ridiculous. He headed toward the barn and to Blue's stall. Leading the horse from his stall, Lucas led him through the barn to the inside corral. He noticed Tinker standing at the rail of the fence. Damn it. What the hell does he want now?

Tinker grinned up at him. "You going to go let some steam off, boss?"

Lucas raised his eyebrows at him. "What makes you say that? I just want to ride."

Tinker laughed. "Yeah, Okay boss. If you say so." He turned away.

"Tinker, you want to explain that?" Lucas glared at him.

Tinker shook his head and laughed. "I don't think it needs explaining." Lucas stared at him. Tinker shrugged. "You're out here cuz that woman's in there." Lucas snorted. "Oh it's true, Lucas. I see how you look at her." He shrugged. "Can't say as I blame you, but be careful. With her husband coming here and looking for trouble, he might think you're in the way."

"Ex," he said. Tinker frowned with obvious confusion. "He's her *ex-husband.*"

Tinker nodded at him. "I know, but I don't want to see anyone get hurt over this, including you."

Lucas sighed as he let Blue run into the corral then motioned for Tinker to follow him to his office. He nodded for Tinker to take a seat. Once they sat down, Lucas reached into the little refrigerator behind the desk and got two beers out. He handed Tinker one and opened one for himself. They both took long pulls on the drink.

"I know how to take care of myself and Emily."

Tinker took a swig from his beer then leaned forward and rested his arms on the desk. "I ain't just talkin' about you gettin' physically hurt and you know it."

Lucas grinned at Tinker. "You think I'm going to get my heart broken, buddy?" Lucas laughed.

Tinker leaned back in his chair. "You think you're immune to it?" Tinker stared at him but Lucas didn't say anything; he sat there smiling. "Let me tell you this Lucas. *Everyone* gets their heart broken sometime in their lifetime. I did a long time ago. And to this day, I wish I hadn't been such an idiot and just married the woman. But you," he pointed at Lucas, "you're already married to the woman. A woman you married without love between you but now that's changed since you're in love with her."

The smile left Lucas's face. He slammed the bottle down on the desk and glared at Tinker. "I am not in love with her," he shouted.

This time Tinker grinned, stood and put both his hands on the desk and glared back at Lucas. "You can tell yourself that all you want, but you and I both know it's a lie."

Lucas stood. The two men stared at each other for a few seconds when Tinker just laughed and picked up his beer. He finished it off and threw the bottle in the trashcan. He winked at Lucas and walked out the door. *Damn it!* Lucas thought.

"You're fired Tinker," he shouted and heard Tinker laugh as he left the barn.

Lucas sat down and shook his head. Tinker was wrong. There was no way he was in love with Emily. They hadn't even been together long, so how could he be in love with her? Tinker was just pulling his chain. They'd gotten to where they teased each other quite a bit and that's all it was. Shaking his head, he left the office, headed back to the house, and entered to find Emily sitting at the table looking through a magazine. She glanced up at him.

"How long is this going to go on?" Lucas asked.

She closed the magazine. "How long is what going to go on?"

Lucas waved his hand between them. "This. Us. Not going to bed. It's been a month."

Her cheeks reddened. "We are getting to know each other, Lucas."

"I know all I need to know. I want you. You're driving me insane," he growled.

"I'm not ready for it yet," Emily whispered.

"Oh, I can get you ready, darlin'," he smirked.

Emily jumped up. "Don't be crude. We agreed to get to know each other first."

"As far as I'm concerned, we have." He took a step toward her.

She backed up. "And as far as I'm concerned, we haven't." She glared up at him. "Are you going to force me, Lucas?"

Lucas halted his forward motion. "I have never forced a woman in my life and I don't intend to start now."

She sighed. "I know. I'm sorry. It was a stupid thing to say."

"We're going to go horseback riding tomorrow and talk. Maybe we can get to know each other. We haven't spent much time together."

Emily nodded. "All right."

"Then when we get back, we're going to bed." At her gasp, he grinned. "Kidding, but hoping." He left the house.

* * * *

Emily blew out a breath when the door closed behind him. It would be very easy to hop into bed with him, but she had to know him better. All she knew is he grew up on the wrong side of the tracks with five of his best friends. He'd left Wyoming only to return five years later. She also knew he was gorgeous and could kiss like a dream but it wasn't enough for her. She needed to *feel* something. Horny wasn't it. She smiled as she headed toward the office when she remembered his words, "I can get you ready." There was no doubt in her mind he could.

The horseback ride didn't happen. There was too much work going on around the ranch. They had several mares coming in season due to artificial light and the stallions were ready to mate. The breeding season started in spring and continued into early fall. A mare could be tricked into season with artificial light. She strolled down the aisle of the barn and listened to the stallions whinnying. They could smell the mares in season. Emily glanced up the aisle and saw Lucas sauntering toward her. He stopped in front of her.

"Are you going to watch the breeding?"

For some reason, she could feel the heat warming her cheeks. She'd seen breeding thousands of times but the thought of watching it with Lucas had her wanting to hide.

"Not this time, I have paperwork to do. Silas Smith wants to buy Sunshine, so I need to get it done for him. He wants to pick her up this weekend." God knows she was rambling but she couldn't help herself. She gazed up at Lucas, he was grinning.

"All right. I understand," he said, all the while grinning. She had a feeling he did understand. Emily spun on her heel to leave. She could hear him coming up behind her. He grabbed her arm and spun her around. Cupping her face in his hands, he lowered his head and pressed his lips to hers. When she opened up to him, he groaned and deepened the kiss. Her arms moved around his neck as he pulled her tighter against him. Suddenly, he let go of her and stepped back. Emily practically ran from the barn.

* * * *

Adam and Stella pulled out from the hotel parking lot. He'd had more than enough of her. Tonight was the night. He was going to get rid of her tonight. As soon as possible. She was driving him up a wall.

"So, we're going to the ranch now?" Stella asked.

Adam bit back a sigh. "We're going to dinner first. I told you already."

Stella giggled and it grated on his nerves. He grit his teeth until they ached. He drove the car along until they came to a dirt road. Adam pulled onto it.

"There's a restaurant down this road?"

Jesus! She was so fucking stupid. "I want to do something first."

"What?"

Adam threw the car into park and reached for her. "Come here."

She smiled. "You want to make out before dinner?"

Adam sneered. "Not quite." He put his hands around her neck and squeezed. Her eyes widened and she tried to claw at his face but he kept her far enough away so she couldn't reach him. She clawed at his arms while trying to breathe. He watched the life go out of her eyes and then he tossed her across the seat. He drove the car a little further down the road. When he came to a place to pull over, he got out, lifted Stella out of the car, and tossed her down over the embankment. He got back into the car and drove back to the motel. No one would miss Stella. She had no family or friends. He'd get rid of her car and get another. Adam hoped some wild animals would get rid of her body. He chuckled as he pulled into the parking lot. After he entered the room, he decided to take a nap. Then he would make his plans for what to do about Emily. He smiled as he laid on the bed and closed his eyes. Soon. He'd have her soon.

* * * *

Two days later, Emily stood at the stove stirring a pot of stew when Lucas walked in the back door. She refused to look at him but she knew he halted at the doorway to the laundry room and glanced over to her. When he walked into the room, she breathed a sigh of relief. It was so hard to block out the reminder of his kiss. She wanted him but she was scared to death. A few minutes went by and he hadn't come back into the kitchen yet. Emily slowly moved to the doorway. She was about to peer in when he came through the doorway. Her nose encountered a hard, naked chest. His arms quickly came up to grasp her arms to keep her from falling backwards. Her hands moved to his solid pecs. Emily slowly raised her eyes to gaze at him and found him staring at her. Her eyes moved to his right arm and she raised a finger to trace the tattoo of an eagle on his bicep. The wing spread out from his shoulder to above his right nipple. Lucas hissed in a breath when her fingers traced it slowly.

"You're playing with fire," he murmured.

Emily raised her eyes. "Am I?"

"I don't think you need me to answer." Lucas slowly lowered his head until his lips were barely touching hers. "But you need to make sure you can handle the heat."

Emily smiled up at him. "I want to find out."

He smiled against her lips. "I do too." He pressed his lips to hers as he picked her up and carried her back into the kitchen.

"I need to turn the stove off," she whispered.

Lucas nodded and strode to the stove. He turned the burner off and then carried her up the stairs. At the top of the landing, he glanced at her. "Which room?"

"You have the bigger bed."

"My bed it is, since I plan on using every inch of it." Lucas chuckled when she blushed. He carried her into the bedroom and laid her down on the bed. Lying down beside her, he cupped her cheek in his palm and lowered his lips to hers. A growl came from deep in his chest when her tongue moved against his. He moved his tongue deep into her mouth, forcing her lips further apart. Lucas moved his hand down her neck to the bottom of her T-shirt. He snaked his hand under it, up to her breast. Emily arched into his hand and moaned into his mouth.

* * * *

Lucas was slowly losing his mind. He wanted to rip her clothes off and take her fast and hard, but he knew he couldn't. Not this time. This time he had to take it slow with her. He wanted to taste every inch of her soft skin. He lifted the shirt over her head and gazed at the red bra. Gritting his teeth, he unhooked the front clasp and groaned when her full breasts fell free. He lowered his head and took a nipple between his teeth. Her fingers clenched fistfuls of his hair. Tugging on the nipple with his teeth until it stood erect, Lucas ran his tongue over it, lapping it before he sucked it into his mouth as he moved his hand down her stomach and unsnapped her jeans. His hand slowly moved inside her panties to between her legs. He slid his finger up and down her wet folds. He was so hard, he ached, but he knew he couldn't rush this.

Lucas rubbed his thumb against her clitoris and inserted a finger inside her. Emily moved against his hand then placed her hand over his and cried out when her orgasm overtook her. Lucas kissed her hard, then stood and removed his clothes, grabbing a condom out of his wallet. He then removed her clothes as she lay panting. He slid between her legs and kissed her. His mouth moved to her neck and down to her breasts again before moving slowly down her stomach. He spread her legs wider and hooked them over his shoulders. His tongue moved between her curls to her clitoris as he inserted two fingers. Lucas gently sucked and rubbed his teeth against her clitoris. He felt her clenching around his fingers as another orgasm hit her. He gazed up at her to see her throw her head back as she shuddered. She reached for him.

"Lucas…please." Emily grabbed the condom from him and rolled it down over his aching shaft. Lucas kissed his way up her body, laid his forehead against hers, and groaned. They gazed into each other's eyes as he slowly inched into her. When he could go no further, they both moaned. Emily's legs encircled his waist. Lucas moved his hand under her to pull her tighter against him and then started to move.

"Move with me Emily," he whispered.

"Kiss me, please." She moaned. "I love how you kiss me."

Lucas pressed his lips to hers and kissed her as they moved together in a rhythm older than time. Never before had it felt this good for him. He didn't want it to end but he so wanted to go over the edge with her.

"Come with me, Emily," he groaned against her lips.

"Yes," she whispered, and tightened her legs around him then cried out as she fell over the edge.

Lucas growled out her name as he followed her. He rested his forehead on hers, both of them breathing hard. Lucas rolled to his side and pulled her against him. Emily rested her head on his chest, her arm slung across his stomach. They fell asleep.

* * * *

Emily woke up and tried to move but a strong arm held her down. She glanced over to see Lucas staring at her. She could feel the blush all over her entire body. She smiled shyly.

"Hey darlin'," Lucas whispered in a husky voice.

"Hey yourself." Emily moved to get up. His arm tightened.

"Where do you think you're going?" Lucas murmured.

"I'd like to take a shower."

"Can I join you?"

Emily moaned. "Oh yes. I'd like that Lucas."

He grinned at her. "Good. I would too." He got out of the bed and held his hand out to her.

Emily did everything she could to keep her eyes on his face but they wandered down his hard chest, six pack stomach to his hard shaft. Her gaze quickly moved back to his face. He shrugged.

"It's your fault." He laughed when she blushed again. "Come on, let's take a shower. I'll even wash your back…and front."

Later in the afternoon, Lucas and Tinker were working in the barn on an old tractor when Emily came into the barn. She smiled at them.

"I think we need to send the men home, Tinker. The weather is calling for a lot of snow. They need to be with their families. You know if it gets too bad, they won't be able to get home."

"I'll tell them to go then," Tinker said and left the barn.

Emily gazed around the barn. Lucas leaned against an old tractor and folded his arms across his chest. "What's wrong?"

"Nothing. Why do you ask?" Emily stared at him.

"You seem nervous."

She sighed. "I just hate sending the men home. The more here the better but with a bad storm moving in, I know they'd want to be with their families."

"I told you I'd protect you. Trust me."

"I do, but…"

Lucas straightened up. "But what? Either you do or you don't." When she didn't say anything, he threw the rag down and headed for the door. "I married you to protect you. If you don't think I can then we shouldn't have done this."

Chapter Four

She watched him go out the door and then she took off running after him. She opened the door and saw him heading to the house. She crouched down, scooped up a handful of snow, and made it in to a snowball. Then with an accuracy that would make the Dodgers proud, she threw it at him, hitting him in the back of the head. His shoulders hunched up when the cold snow hit him. She watched as he slowly turned around to face her. She reached down quickly and formed another snowball, tossing it up and down when he looked at her.

He put his hands on his hips, "Did you just hit me with a snowball?"

Emily tried not to laugh. "Maybe." She watched him standing there glaring at her before he reached down, picked up snow, formed a ball, and started striding toward her. She backed up. He came forward and had a grin on his face. She had to tease him, "Do you have to get closer to hit me with it? Can't do it from there?" She snickered.

He laughed. "Who said I was going to throw it at you? Maybe I'm going to rub it in your face."

She gasped and took off for the barn door behind her. The snowball hit the door as she swung it open. Glancing over her shoulder, she saw him scooping up more snow. She ran into the barn. Lucas came in right behind her, caught her, and tackled her to the floor. She screamed and struggled but he was much stronger. He had her on her back in no time and laid on top of her. He pinned her hands above her head with one hand. Emily was laughing so hard she had tears running down her cheeks as she was shaking her head back and forth trying to keep him from smearing the snowball on her face. He was holding it over her face.

"Say you're sorry." he demanded. She shook her head no. He let go of her hands and grabbed her chin to stop her. She opened her eyes and gazed up at him. He was staring at her lips.

"Lucas," she whispered.

His eyes closed as he leaned down to kiss her. Running his tongue along her lips, he whispered, "Always open for me, baby." She allowed him access and moaned into his mouth. She could feel his arousal pressing against her leg. He groaned into her mouth, tore his lips from hers, and ran his mouth along her jaw to her ear, nipping her earlobe with his teeth. He brought his mouth back to her lips. He nudged her knees apart, settled between them, and then moved against her. She moved against him. He stopped kissing her.

"Emily, open your eyes and look at me," Lucas whispered.

She opened her eyes slowly and stared into his gorgeous face. He smiled at her and she smiled back and moved to put her arms around his neck. She forgot about the snowball in her gloved hand. It slipped down his neck. He yelped and jumped up. She was laughing watching him try to get the snow off the back of his neck. He looked down at her.

"You are in so much trouble now, woman." He narrowed his eyes at her.

She laughed up at him. "Promises, promises."

He put a hand out to her. She took it and he pulled her to her feet.

"That was quicker than a cold shower," he told her.

She looked up at him. "How many of those have you ever had?" she teased.

He burst out laughing, "Before we ended up in bed, I took one every night since I've been here." She put her hand over her mouth. He looked at her grinning. "Did you think I was going to lie about it?" She shook her head. He reached for her hand and squeezed it in his. "Let's go in. I need to get a hot shower. Damn snow down my back."

Emily laughed. "Would you like me to wash the snow off your back?"

"I believe it will melt by the time we get to the house but you can still wash my back."

Emily grinned up at him. "Can I wash your front too?"

Lucas groaned. "Hell yes."

Emily laughed. "I just might let you return the favor."

Lucas pulled her against him and kissed her. "You're killing me," he whispered against her lips.

"I don't want to do that. I need you to protect me."

"I will." Lucas kissed her quick. "I promise."

"I know you will. I don't doubt it Lucas. It's just if there were more people here Adam wouldn't do anything."

"He's not going to do anything anyway. The storm will keep him away for now."

Emily nodded. "Yes. For now."

Lucas put his arm around her shoulders and led her from the barn. "Let's get a shower and try to think of a way to spend the rest of the day."

Emily halted and gazed up at him. She narrowed her eyes. "I'm sure we can think of something."

"You must be thinking what I'm thinking." Lucas grinned.

Emily strolled ahead of him. "Yes. Monopoly sounds fun." She took off running when he growled and reached for her. He was right on her heels as they ran into the house. Lucas grabbed her around the waist and tossed her over his shoulder. Emily squealed.

"Monopoly my ass," he told her. "We're going to the bedroom."

"The game's in the closet," she said, laughing.

Lucas smacked her butt. "If you want to play a game I know one. It's called 'let's get naked'."

"Hmmm. I've never played that one. Sounds fun." Emily reached down and squeezed his butt, making him growl.

"Again, she plays with fire."

Emily laughed. She was in trouble. Falling in love wasn't in the mix but she was doing it anyway. He was her husband after all, and he made her feel safe. If only he loved her too. The good thing was he wanted to stay married, she was thankful for that. Once Adam was out of her life, she wanted to have a baby. A family is what she wanted with Lucas. He carried her into the bedroom, lowered her to the bed, and leaned over her.

"How about a shower now?" he murmured against her lips.

"I thought we were going to play 'let's get naked'"?" She smiled.

His lips rose in a slow smile. "Darlin', have you forgotten you have to get naked to shower?"

Emily pressed her lips to his. "So, this game can be played anywhere?"

"Anywhere. Anytime." Lucas took her hand and pulled her to her feet then led her to the bathroom. He turned the shower on and turned to her. Cupping her face in his hands, he kissed her slowly. Emily sighed against his lips.

Lucas lifted her shirt and tossed it to the floor; her bra followed. He knelt in front of her, unsnapped her jeans, and lowered them along with her panties. She stepped from them and stood naked in front of him. He wrapped his arms around her waist, pulled her to him, kissed her belly, and moved down to her curls. His tongue moved through them, her hands fisted in his hair. He lifted her leg over his shoulder as he feasted on her. She began to shake then cried out his name. Lucas stood and shed his clothes. He led her into the shower. Emily wrapped her hand around his hard shaft, making him groan. Lucas tried to push her hand away but she shook her head, got on her knees in front of him, and kissed the head of his shaft. He groaned and ran his fingers through her hair. Emily took him in her mouth and ran her tongue along the length. She gently sucked and moved her hand to the base and pumped. Lucas's hips arched forward when all of a sudden, he lifted her up, put her back against the wall and her legs around his waist. He started to inch into her slowly.

"God, you kill me when you do that." Emily groaned.

Lucas chuckled. "I kill myself when all I want to do is take you hard and fast."

"Then do it." He slammed into her making her gasp. "Yes," she cried out.

Lucas moved hard and fast against her. Emily held onto him, nipping his neck. All of a sudden, he pulled out of her.

"What are you doing?" She exclaimed.

"I don't have a condom on."

"I'm on the pill. Come on," Emily growled.

Lucas burst out laughing. "Awful damn demanding." He thrust back into her, making them both groan. He pummeled into her over and over until he felt her muscles tighten around him. She screamed out when her orgasm hit her. Lucas groaned and came with her.

"Don't let go of me," she whispered.

"Never." He kissed her forehead. Then he carried her from the shower and dried her off, then himself. They laid on the bed holding each other, lost in their own thoughts. Emily could feel her eyelids getting heavy. Her last thought before falling asleep was he said 'never'.

* * * *

An hour later, Lucas brushed her bangs from her forehead. She opened her eyes and smiled at him.

"You're so beautiful, Emily," he whispered.

"Lucas…"

"You are. Don't deny it. I love your green eyes, your long dark hair. The first time I saw it down I almost wept. It's gorgeous. I hate seeing it up."

"I have to wear it up when I'm working. It gets in my way."

Lucas nodded. "I know, but when you're done for the day, I want it down, and I especially want it down when you're here with me. In bed."

Emily grinned. "Yes, sir."

Lucas gave a breathless laugh. "Good." He cleared his throat. "Tell me about your ex-husband." He felt her stiffen. "I think it's time you told me."

Emily scooched up against the headboard with the sheet under her arms. "I met Adam when I was nineteen years old. He was older, smart, and handsome. I was flattered he was interested in me. He loved me, I don't doubt it, but he had a strange way of showing it. My grandfather hated him and I should've listened to him when he told me Adam was the wrong man for me." She shook her head. "I literally ran into him in town. I was coming out of the bank and he was going in. I almost knocked him down the steps. Of course, I couldn't apologize enough and he said the only way he'd forgive me is if I joined him for dinner. With him being a stranger in town, I was leery, but agreed to meet him at the diner." She huffed. "So, the romance began. We married when I was twenty."

"What did he do for a living?"

"He worked at a bank, as a manager. He'd just been transferred here."

Lucas sat up. "From where?"

"Casper."

"He came from a big city bank to work here? Sounds suspicious to me."

Emily nodded. "Yes, my grandfather thought the same. We later found out the bank gave Adam the option of working here or leave the bank, including all branches. There were rumors he'd been extorting from bank customers and embezzling. Seems like they weren't rumors since he was caught doing the same thing here."

"How long were you married?"

"Three years when he was sent to prison. By then, I hated him. He belittled me constantly. Every day he'd tell me how stupid I was and he was the only man who would ever want me. I believed him. When you hear it enough, it starts to sink in that's how everyone sees you. I thought he was right and no other man would ever want me. It took me a long time to know it was his way of making me stay with him. My grandfather built us a home close to town since Adam refused to live on the ranch. He hates horses. My father wouldn't even speak to him. My grandfather, however, told him constantly what a waste of human flesh he was."

Lucas laughed. "I always liked your grandfather. He gave me a job here when no one else wanted anything to do with me."

Emily ran her fingers through his hair. "I know. I had the biggest crush on you."

"I know you did, but your dad didn't like me at all. He thought I was trouble and he was right. I was."

"Tell me about your childhood."

"Finish with your ex first."

Emily sighed. "Not much more to tell. The FBI arrested him for extortion. He expected my family to help him out but they refused and by then I was so glad to be away from him, there was no way I wanted to help him stay out of prison." She glanced away and swallowed hard. "He swore he'd never let me go. I had to fight him for a divorce and he told me I'd regret it. We were married until death do us part and he'd make sure that's how it ended."

"Not exactly a death threat but you know it's what he meant."

"Yes. The only thing I could do was get a restraining order but it won't stop him. He's going to come after me."

Lucas pulled her to him and wrapped his arms around her. "I'll be waiting for him." At that moment, Munch jumped up on the bed and stared at Lucas. "Yeah, I don't like you either, cat."

Emily laughed. "You two will get used to each other. I have to feed her."

Lucas wouldn't let her up. "What about me? I'm hungry."

"Sure. What do you want?"

Lucas slid lower in the bed, pulling her down with him. "You." Munch had to wait.

* * * *

Two days later, the snow finally let up. Emily sat in the front window seat staring out. She heard the back door open and her heart slammed into her ribs. She knew Lucas just came in. He came striding into the living room and halted when he saw her.

"Anything wrong?" he asked as he moved toward her.

She shook her head. "No. I was just daydreaming."

"About me?" He grinned.

She laughed softly. "Of course." Munch jumped up beside her and glared at Lucas.

Lucas sat down and pushed Munch off the cushion. The cat hissed at him. He chuckled and pulled Emily's ponytail. "The weather is supposed to warm up."

"I know."

"We're ready for him, darlin'." Lucas leaned forward and kissed her.

"I want you to tell me about your childhood, Lucas. You got out of it the other day."

He raised his eyebrows. "I did?"

She playfully punched him. "You know you did. I want to know all about you."

Lucas huffed. "How about tonight? I still have things to do this afternoon."

Emily agreed and watched him leave the room and then heard the back door closing behind him. She knew he wasn't real proud of his childhood and teenage years but she knew a lot of it, she just wanted to hear his version. Munch jumped up on her lap again.

"Hello pretty girl. Are you tolerating Lucas?" Emily was happy when Munch didn't growl. She continued to pet Munch until the cat curled into a ball and fell asleep. Emily laid down and closed her eyes.

* * * *

Lucas found her a couple of hours later. He walked softly toward her and squatted down. He brushed her hair off her face. Her eyes opened slowly.

"Hi darlin'," he whispered right before he kissed her.

Emily smiled against his lips. "Hi. What time is it?"

"Almost six."

Emily jumped up. "I haven't even started dinner."

"It's fine. Let me get a shower and we'll go into town for dinner."

"Are you sure?"

"Why not? We've both been stuck on this ranch for weeks. Let's go out." Lucas stood and gazed down at her.

"I'd like that." Emily grinned and started toward the stairs. "But I need a shower first." She ran up the stairs. Lucas right behind her.

"We'll conserve water and shower together." He laughed as he caught her and carried her the rest of the way. Dinner was very late.

Lucas jerked awake later, and quickly glanced around the room. It was past midnight but the full moon lit the room enough to see nothing was amiss. He was about to close his eyes when he heard voices. He quietly got out of bed and moved to the window.

"*Shit!*" He moved to pull his jeans on.

"What is it?" Emily asked.

"The horses are out of the barn." Lucas ran from the room.

"What?" Emily squealed as she quickly dressed and ran out the door behind him. She caught up to him in the kitchen. Lucas grabbed her and sat her on a chair.

"Stay here." He pulled his coat on.

"I'm going out there, Lucas."

"No! It could be a diversion to get you outside. You will stay in this house and lock the door behind me." He grasped her arms. "Do you understand?"

She nodded. "Yes." She grabbed his arm when he turned from her. "Please...be careful."

Lucas kissed her quickly and ran outside and toward the men. They were trying to corral the horses but the animals were scared. Tinker glanced over at him.

"I hope none of them took off for the pastures."

"How long have they been out?"

"About fifteen minutes is all." Tinker nodded his head toward the road.

"Any idea how they got out?" Lucas asked.

"Not yet," Tinker told him.

"I have an idea," Lucas muttered. Tinker stared at him and nodded.

Lucas and Tinker moved about helping the men round up the horses. Once they were back in the barn, Lucas did a head count. Two were missing.

"I can send Jack and Eric out to look," Tinker suggested.

"It's too damn dark and I don't want them out there as cold as it is. The horses shouldn't go anywhere but the pastures. We'll look in the morning."

"All right, but one of the missing is Emily's horse, Cinnamon. I wouldn't tell her if I were you. She'd want to go looking for her."

Lucas nodded. "You're right. It may be warming up during the day but at night, it's still frigid and I don't want anyone out there after dark. Maybe the horses will come back by morning." He slapped Tinker on the shoulder. "You and the men get back to bed. I'll see you first thing."

Tinker nodded. "Are you sure you don't want one of us to keep an eye out?"

"I don't think he'll come back tonight but he's shown his hand now. We'll keep an eye out." Neither man had to say who they thought it was causing trouble. They knew it was Adam letting them know he was around.

Tinker sighed and strode off. Lucas knew Tinker wanted to keep an eye out but Lucas was sure Adam was just getting started. Things were going to get much worse before they got better. Lucas clenched his fists. He wanted a shot at the coward. Just one shot.

Early the next morning, Lucas rode Blue out of the barn and saw Emily standing on the porch. He knew the minute she saw him, he galloped the horse over to her.

"Hi." He smiled at her.

She smiled. "Where are you going?"

Lucas shifted in the saddle. "Two horses were left out last night."

"*What?*" She practically shouted. "Why didn't you tell me this last night?"

"Because I knew you'd want to go out looking for them and it was too dark and too damn cold."

"So you just decided not to tell me at all?" Emily placed her hands on her hips and glared at him.

"I just told you, didn't I?"

"Only because I asked. Damn it Lucas. You don't have the option of not telling me something like that."

"Do I or do I not own half this ranch?" He leaned forward.

"You do but as a partnership, we need to let each other know when something like this happens."

"You wouldn't have slept, Emily. I'm sure they're fine." He tuned the reins to move away.

"What horses are they?"

He sighed. "Star Gazer and Cinnamon."

"Cinnamon is missing? You should have told me last night." She ran back into the house and came back out with her coat.

"What are you doing?" Lucas asked her.

She glared up at him. "That is my horse and I'm going after her. I can't believe you didn't tell me this." She marched to the barn and disappeared inside. A few minutes later, she came back out on horseback and after giving him a glare, she nudged the horse into a run out through the yard. Lucas swore and tore off after her. The woman could ride, that was for sure. Lucas caught up to her, reached over, and grabbed the reins, halting her horse. Emily jerked them from him.

"You need to slow the hell down," he roared.

"I know every inch of this land and I know how to ride." She jerked the horse away and tore off again.

"*Son of a bitch!*" Lucas nudged Blue and ran him full speed until he caught up with her. This time, he reached over and pulled her off the horse and across his lap.

"Put me down," Emily screamed.

Lucas stopped his horse. "Not until you settle down." He sighed. "Look, I'm sorry but Tinker and I both made the call not to tell you last night. It was mostly my decision but we didn't want you out here in the dark looking for your horse. If you'd just calm down and think, you'd admit I'm right."

She quit struggling and nodded. "I know you're right. It's just that I've had her since she was a year old and she's fifteen now. I hate it that she spent the night out here as cold as it is."

Lucas kissed her. "We'll find her. Now. If I put you back on your horse, you're not going to take off are you?"

"No. I'll ride alongside you."

He gave her a nod, rode her over to her horse, and sat her on the saddle. She smiled at him. Lucas rolled his eyes and shook his head. They rode the horses through the north pasture and didn't see the other horses yet. They headed to the west pasture and spotted them. Lucas heard Emily let out a sigh. She glanced over to him and smiled. His heart hit his stomach.

"See? They're both fine." He tried to swallow the lump in his throat.

"Yes. Let's get them home." She rode her horse closer and dismounted.

Lucas watched as she slowly moved toward the two horses. Her horse, Cinnamon walked right toward her. The other horse followed. Cinnamon butted her head against Emily's chest. Emily laughed and rubbed her ears.

"Let's go home, girl." Emily said as she slipped a rope over Cinnamon's head then she mounted her horse and they rode home.

Chapter Five

As the April weather began warming the earth, Emily grew more fearful. She knew Adam was out there, even though nothing more had happened in the past two weeks. He was waiting for the perfect opportunity to make his move. She stood staring out the window in the office. The snow was almost gone. Brown grass was beginning to push through what snow remained and she knew it would soon turn green. It wouldn't be long before daffodils sprouted up. Sighing, she headed for the kitchen to get a cup of tea. The back door opened and Lucas walked in as she entered the room. He took his hat off and reached her in a few strides. He cupped her face in his palms and kissed her.

"Hi," he said against her lips.

"Hi yourself." She smiled up at him. "What are you doing in here?"

"I wanted to see you." He pressed his lips to hers and deepened the kiss.

Emily moaned then pulled back. "You have work to do, Mister Taggart."

Lucas laughed. "I'd rather do you, Missus Taggart."

Emily gasped. "You did not come in here for that…did you?"

He chuckled. "No but it doesn't mean I wouldn't be up for it. Literally."

She swatted at him. "You're awful." Emily moved to the stove when the teapot whistled. "Do you want me to make you some coffee?"

"No. I came in to talk to you about Joe. I think he deserves a raise."

"Joe Truman?" At his nod, Emily went on. "If you think he deserves a raise, you don't need to talk to me about it."

"No?" Lucas sighed and ran his fingers through his thick hair. "I guess I'm just not used to being in charge."

Emily moved closer to him and wrapped her arms around his waist. "You are, though. We're in this together. This is half your ranch. Remember that."

Lucas grinned. "Yes ma'am." He winked as he picked his hat up and walked out.

Emily shook her head and after getting her tea, headed to the office to work on the books and sales coming up.

* * * *

Two days later, Emily and Lucas drove into town to pick up feed and she needed to visit the bank. "We're supposed to get more snow tonight." She shook her head. "I thought we were done with it."

Lucas sighed. "Yeah, I know. I'll be glad when winter's over."

"That could be June." Emily laughed.

Lucas glanced over to her. "Not funny."

She chuckled. "We do live in northern Wyoming."

"Well, if we get stranded inside, we'll just stay in bed and while away the hours some way." He winked at her, then chuckled when she blushed.

"You love to embarrass me, Lucas." She folded her arms across her chest and stuck her bottom lip out.

"I love to see you blush. Even though we're married, you still blush when I mention sex in any way." He pointed at her. "See? There it is again."

Emily laughed. "I hate you."

Lucas shook his head. "I sure hope not darlin'. I sure hope not."

They pulled in to the feed store and walked inside. A few of the patrons waved but others stared at them as if they couldn't understand why Emily would marry him. Lucas took a deep breath, and strode to the counter.

"We need ten fifty-pound bags of oats for the horses," Lucas told the man behind the counter. The man stared at him for a few seconds then shifted his eyes to Emily.

"Give him anything he wants, Carl. Anytime Lucas comes in here, you take his order and fill it," Emily told him.

Lucas clenched his jaw and stared at Carl, who turned from the counter to place the order. He felt Emily's hand on his arm.

"You won't have a problem if you come in alone the next time," she said.

"They're all wondering why you married someone like me," Lucas muttered.

"It doesn't matter what they think, does it? We're married and it's none of their business," she whispered.

Lucas nodded. "If you say so."

Emily grabbed the sleeve of his coat. "Lucas Taggart, you listen to me. I don't care what any of them think my reasons for marrying you are." She glared up at him.

He glanced down into her face and she knew he saw truth and determination. He grinned. "All right."

"I'm going to go to the bank while you get the feed." She stood on her toes and kissed his cheek. He grinned at her.

She was strolling down the sidewalk toward the bank when she heard her name. Stopping, she looked over her shoulder and smiled.

"Hello Mr. Danvers."

Harley Danvers was the president of the Bank of Dry River. She did all her business with him.

"Hello Emily. How are you honey?" His bushy mustache covered most of his teeth when he smiled.

"I'm just fine. I was actually heading for the bank to make a deposit and pay off the loan."

"Well, then do me the honor of accompanying me." He stuck his elbow out for her to take. She looped her hand through his arm and strolled along with him. "It looks like more snow is moving in again."

Emily glanced at him. He seemed nervous. "What is it?"

Harley stopped and stared at her. "Adam was in yesterday. He came waltzing into the bank, walked around, and then left. Never said a word to anyone. Just strutted like a peacock." Emily felt the blood drain from her face. Harley patted her hand. "You didn't know he was back?"

"I thought he was back. It's just hearing he's actually here, is too real."

Harley led her into the bank and his office. He had her sit while he got her a cup of water. He handed it to her and sat behind his desk. "Are you all right, Emily?"

She nodded but sipped the water. "I'll be fine."

"Is there someone I could call for you? You look a little pale."

Emily shook her head but reached into her purse and pulled her cell phone out. She glanced at Harley. "I'll call Lucas. He's down at the feed store."

Harley nodded. "Is there anything I can do for you while you wait for him?"

"Just pay the loan off."

"You're sure you want to do that?"

"Yes. We sold two horses this week."

"All right. I'll get the papers." He walked around the desk and put his hand on her shoulder. "I'll be right back. Call Lucas."

Emily's hand was shaking as she held her phone. She dialed Lucas's number.

"Hello darlin'. You miss me already?" He chuckled.

"Lucas…" Her voice cracked.

"Emily? What is it?" She could hear the panic in his voice.

"I'm at the bank. Harley told me Adam was in here yesterday."

"Stay there. I'm on my way." Lucas hung up.

Emily sat in the wingback chair and stared at the phone. He'd be there soon and then she'd feel safe. Lucas would keep her safe. She dropped the phone into her purse and folded her arms. She couldn't seem to get warm as she rubbed her hands up and down her arms. Harley came back into the office.

"Did you call Lucas? Is he coming here?"

She nodded. "He should be here in a few minutes."

Harley sat at his desk and laid the papers out for her to sign. Emily knew he was trying to keep her occupied until Lucas got there. Harley handed her a pen but she sat there staring at the papers. She raised her eyes to look at him and she knew he could see the fear in them.

"Lucas will be here soon," Harley said softly.

Emily sat on the edge of her seat and signed the papers then she pulled out a checkbook and wrote a check for the balance of the loan. Her hand was shaking so badly, she had trouble holding onto the pen. She finally signed it, tore the check out, and handed it to Harley. He took it from her and then squeezed her hand. At that moment, Lucas came through the door and then squatted down in front of her.

"Hey darlin'," he whispered.

Emily stared at him for a few seconds before a sob tore from her throat as she launched herself at him.

"He's really here. I know we thought he was when the horses were let out but people have actually seen him, Lucas."

"I know, baby. Let's go home. I'll take care of you." Lucas kissed her forehead then glanced at Harley. "Is there anything else she needs to do about the loan?"

"No. I'll mail you the papers showing the loan's paid off. Just take her home, Lucas."

Lucas shook Harley's hand and helped her walk out of the bank to their truck. After helping her in, he walked around and got in. She glanced over to him. He put the truck in drive and headed home.

* * * *

As Lucas drove toward the ranch, his gaze moved from the rearview mirror to Emily. She stared straight ahead. He didn't want to alarm her but he was sure there was a car following them. It pulled out behind them in town but stayed back far enough so he couldn't see the driver or the front license plate. Not wanting to scare Emily, he reached for her hand. She turned scared eyes to him.

"Don't turn around but I think we're being followed."

She quickly glanced in the side mirror. "The black car behind us?"

"No. The red one behind it. He's been following since we left the bank but staying back far enough to not make him out. I think he deliberately let the black car between us." Lucas shook his head. "I don't like it."

"It's Adam," she said with certainty.

Lucas's jaw clenched. "I'm sure it is too." He swore under his breath. "I'd love to have a conversation with him. Man to man."

Emily snorted. "He's not a man. He's a snake who slithers around to scare people."

A burst of laughter erupted from Lucas. "He doesn't scare me."

"You're probably the only one then."

Lucas swerved the truck off the road and parked it on the berm. His eyes never left the mirror as the red car approached then slowly passed by. The tinted windows didn't allow him to see the driver. He pulled out behind the car and followed it.

"What are you doing?" Emily asked.

"Just giving him some of his own medicine."

The car sped up but Lucas stayed with him. Emily touched his arm. He glanced over to her.

"Please don't. It will just make him angry."

"I want the son of a bitch angry. I want him to come after me."

"Lucas, please."

He sighed and let off the gas then pulled off the road and shoved the truck into park. He laid his arm along the back of the seat. "He's pushing it, Emily and he knows it. Walking into the bank he used to work at then following us. He's going to get more and more brazen as time goes on. I want him to know I'm not afraid of him."

"I don't want you to get hurt." She slid across to sit beside him and put her hand on his cheek. "Please don't antagonize him. He'll only come after us with more anger and his anger is not something to mess with."

"I told you, I'm not afraid of him. I want him to come after me, not you."

"He's only interested in me and if he thinks for one second you'll be in the way, he'll do what he can to get rid of you. One way or another, he'll get rid of you. I know him. Trust me on this." She sighed. "It's why we're better staying together. In town or at the ranch. He won't try to get to me with you at my side but if he can separate us, he will and then he'll make his move. What were you planning to do by following him?"

Lucas grumbled. "I have no idea. I just wanted to let him know I'm not worried about him."

Emily kissed his cheek and slid back across the seat. "He doesn't care you're not worried. It's me he's after."

Lucas nodded and didn't say anymore. The thought of Adam trying to intimidate them was something he wanted to change. Lucas wanted to talk with him, convince him to let Emily alone. He pulled up to the house and turned to her.

"Where does he get money if he just got out of prison?"

"His parents were stinking rich. They both died within the last two years. Adam inherited everything. I don't understand why he wanted my family to help with his felony charge when his parents had money." She shook her head. "Anyway, there was no other family. Since he was in prison, the money sat in a bank and drew interest. He has enough money to buy anything or anyone he wants. Which is why I wanted a man I thought wouldn't care about the money I know he'll offer."

Lucas narrowed his eyes at her. "You think he'll offer me money?"

Emily laughed without humor. "Oh yes. He'll contact you in some way and offer you money for me. I can promise you that."

"Why didn't you tell me this before?"

She shrugged. "Because I know you don't care about the money. You've got a partnership in a very lucrative ranch, why would you need the money?"

Lucas nodded. "True but some people never seem to have enough."

Emily moved closer to him. "But you're not one of them, Lucas. I can tell you love the work, not the money it brings. After talking with your mother, I knew you were the one I wanted protecting me."

He muttered under his breath. "I can't believe you talked to my mom about this."

Emily laughed. "Let's go inside. I don't like being out here."

Lucas nodded and pulled her out the door of the truck and led her inside. They took their jackets off and Emily went about making dinner. Lucas headed to the office to work on the books. He couldn't concentrate. The thoughts of Adam attempting to bribe him set him on edge. Lucas hoped he did try so he could laugh in his face. There wasn't enough money in the world to make him give up Emily. He sat back in the chair and stared out the window at his land. His and Emily's. He wanted to see their children out there running around the yard in the summer and building a snowman in the winter. He wanted to teach them to ride horses and love them as he did. They'd grow up learning the trade of raising and selling the best Quarter horses money could buy.

Lucas sat forward and rested his arms on the desk. When had she come to mean so much to him? He woke up every morning, looked over at her, and wanted nothing more than to pull her close and hold her. He thought of her all day long while he was in the barn with the men. Sometimes he'd catch Tinker smiling at him and Lucas would glare at him until Tinker would chuckle and walk off. Lucas laughed softly. Tinker knew Lucas was a goner where Emily was concerned, although, he still wouldn't admit he was in love with her. She never said how she felt about him and he wasn't putting his heart out there. He wanted them to make the marriage work and have babies together. Dark haired, green-eyed babies. Beautiful like their mommy.

Lucas reached for the phone and called his good friend, Montgomery Bradford. Mont was an FBI agent out of the Jackson Hole office. They'd grown up together in Dry River. Mont was one of the "bad boys" too. After asking for him, Lucas sat and waited for his friend to come on the line and prayed Emily didn't come back to the office.

"This is Agent Bradford, can I help you?"

Lucas chuckled. "Still gets me hearing you call yourself an agent."

Masculine laughter came across the line. "Lucas. How are you?"

"Good Mont, you?"

"You're not good or you wouldn't be calling me."

Lucas sighed. "You know me too well. I have a little problem I'm hoping you can give me some advice on."

"I'll try. What is it?"

Lucas explained about Emily and her ex-husband. About him showing up and following them.

"Wait. You got married?" Mont asked in disbelief.

"Another long story but suffice it to say, I married her to protect her from her ex."

"Yeah right. Tell me another one."

"I got half her horse ranch."

"Now the truth comes out. Big ranch?"

"Whispering Pines."

"Holy shit." Mont yelled. "You own half of Whispering Pines?"

"It was part of the deal. Look, Mont. I'll be more than happy to explain some other time but right now, I want to know if there's any way we can get him away from here and Emily."

"Not really. He hasn't done anything wrong. You can't even prove he was following you and even if he was, he could say he was heading that way too. He hasn't broken any laws. Have you talked with Nathan about it?"

"No. Like you said, he hasn't done anything...yet."

"You think he will?"

"Yes. He wants to hurt her, I'm sure of it. She seems to think he'll offer me money to leave her or hand her over."

"Jesus. What a nice guy. Look, you know my hands are tied. I can give you advice as a friend but I can't help you with things like that. Unless he takes her, I can't be involved."

Lucas ran his hand down his face. "Shit. I know. I just wanted your opinion. I'll talk to you soon. After all this shit is over, come visit and meet my wife."

Mont burst out laughing. "I never thought I'd ever hear you say that. Later."

Lucas hung up, glanced at the door, and groaned. Emily stood there staring at him.

"Who was that?" she asked as she entered the room.

"Mont."

"Montgomery Bradford?" She sat in the chair across from him.

"Yes. Although, he never goes by Montgomery. You know Mont too?"

"I know *of* him. I never knew any of the boys you ran with." She smiled. "The bad boys of Dry River."

Lucas moaned. "Please don't say that."

Emily laughed. "It's true. All of you had a reputation. All the girls had crushes on you and later all the women wanted you." She leaned forward. "I had a crush on you when I was seven."

Lucas grinned. "Yes, I know. You already mentioned it."

Emily blushed. "You carried me home. I'll never forget it. Anyway, why were you calling Montgomery?"

"He's an FBI agent now." Lucas watched her eyes widen and laughed. "Yeah, shock, huh?"

Emily shook her head. "I can't believe it. From bad boy to FBI agent."

"I called him to see if there's anything we can do about Walters but Mont said since Walters hasn't done anything, there isn't." Lucas stood and strolled around the desk and squatted down in front of her. "The restraining order will help."

"I don't think it will. A piece of paper isn't going to keep him from me."

"Probably not, but it's the principal of the thing. If he comes anywhere near you, we can have him arrested," Lucas told her.

"Mont thinks I should tell Nathan about Walters."

"The sheriff? I forgot about you knowing Nathan. Being one of your best friend's brothers, it makes sense you'd know him." Emily stood and moved toward the window. "I just want Adam to leave me alone. I can't offer him money because he has more than God so it wouldn't matter to him." She folded her arms and turned to face Lucas. "We're in a wait and see situation."

Lucas moved toward her and wrapped his arms around her. "I won't let him get to you."

"For how long though? How long will we have to keep this up?"

"Keep what up? Our marriage?" Lucas clenched his jaw as he gazed down at her.

"No. How long will we have to keep looking around every corner? I thought you said you wanted to stay married?"

"I do. I just thought you meant you wanted to end it once we were rid of him."

"Lucas, I want to stay married to you. I...like being married to you, even if it is a little unconventional." She smiled up at him.

He pulled her into his arms. "I like being married to you too. It is unconventional but I like the benefits." He chuckled when she blushed.

* * * *

Emily hugged him tighter. She was so scared of Adam getting to her. Lucas would do all he could to protect her but he couldn't be with her twenty four seven. There were days he spent hours in the barn. All Adam had to do was get to know their routine. She may hate the man but she also knew he was smart and had plenty of money to hire anyone to do his bidding. Emily shivered against Lucas. His arms tightened around her. She'd die if something happened to him. Falling in love with her husband happened so quickly, it shocked her. How can you fall in love with someone so fast? Emily pulled back and gazed up at him.

"I don't want you to get hurt, Lucas," she whispered.

"I won't. I can handle myself."

"You don't know him. He's ruthless." Emily hugged him again. "He won't stop until he makes me pay for divorcing him. He always said he'd never let me go."

"He doesn't have a choice. You're married to me now and he needs to get over it."

Emily knew that wouldn't happen. Adam was hell bent on making her pay for divorcing him. He was obsessed with her and always had been. He belittled her to make her think no other man would ever want her. Now Lucas was her husband and Emily knew with all her heart Adam would never accept it.

* * * *

Two weeks later, Adam sat across from the feed store and watched as Lucas Taggart carried out a bag of salt as if it weighed nothing. The man was big and strong. Adam had his work cut out for him. If he approached him, he was sure Taggart would punch him. Sighing, he pulled out his cell phone and dialed the number on the feed store sign. When someone answered, he asked to speak to Taggart. He heard them lay the phone down and a minute later, Adam saw a young woman run out the door and talk with Taggart. He put the salt bag into the bed of the truck and followed her inside.

"This is Lucas."

"I want to meet with you," Adam said. A silence greeted him. "This is—"

"I know who it is. When?"

"Now. I'm across the street."

The next thing Adam knew, someone pulled him from the car and then slammed him back against it. Lucas glared at him. He was much taller than he looked from across the street. Lucas put his face close.

"What the fuck do you want, Walters?"

Adam pushed his hands away and straightened his suit jacket. "I think you know what I want." Lucas raised an eyebrow. Adam sighed. "I want my wife."

Lucas laughed. "Your wife? You don't have a wife. Emily is married to me now."

Adam clenched his jaw. "Nonetheless. I want her. I'm prepared to offer you a lot of money."

"You don't have enough," Lucas told him.

"Everyone has a price. Name yours."

"I don't have one when it comes to my wife. I have everything I need."

"I can make you a very rich man." Lucas stepped back and glared at him. Adam smiled. "Very rich indeed."

Lucas folded his arms across his chest. "How rich we talking?"

"A few million," Adam grinned.

"A few million? That's it? Whispering Pines is worth way more than that."

"I can give you whatever you want. Ten million," Adam sneered.

"And all I have to do is hand Emily over to you?"

"You hand her over, you get the money, and you keep Whispering Pines."

"I already have Whispering Pines. I have enough money and I will not hand Emily over to you. Ever." Lucas opened the car door and shoved Adam inside. "Now get the hell out of here and if I see you anywhere near her, you'll deal with me. I'm not afraid of you."

Adam watched as he slammed the car door closed and strode across the street. He got into his truck and pulled out. Adam gripped the steering wheel until his knuckles turned white. He needed to take the bastard out and soon. He was going to need some help and he knew just the men to call. Friends he'd made in prison who were out now too. Adam would have to deal with Lucas Taggart but first he had to get Emily away from him.

* * * *

Son of a bitch! Lucas slammed his fist against the steering wheel. The bastard had balls, he'd give him that. Ten million? Lucas wouldn't take any amount to hand Emily over. Her life wasn't measured in money nor were his feelings for her. Did Walters think money was the cure-all for anything and everything? Shaking his head, he was still shocked he'd been offered money for his wife. For what? What did Walters have in mind for her? Was he going to kill her or just run off with her? Did he seriously think Emily would willingly go away with him? Or did it even matter to him one way or the other? Lucas knew the answer. It didn't matter to Walters how Emily felt, it was what he wanted that mattered.

"Damn it," he shouted. Emily told him Walters would offer him money, he just found it hard to believe. He pulled onto the road leading to Whispering Pines and felt a sense of pride knowing he was part owner. It was enough for him. He shared it with his wife and hopefully one day, their children.

Pulling up to the back door, he hopped out and strolled inside. The house seemed eerily quiet. He removed his jacket and hat then walked through the kitchen to the living room. Emily wasn't there so he headed down the hall toward the office. He opened the door and saw the room was empty. Spinning on his heel, he ran for the stairs and took them two at a time until he reached their room. He slowly pushed the door open and breathed a sigh of relief when he saw her lying on the bed, asleep.

Lucas moved toward the bed and sat down on it. He brushed her hair from her cheek. Her eyes fluttered open and she gazed up at him and smiled.

"Hi," she whispered.

"Hi. Are you feeling all right? You rarely take naps." His hand caressed her cheek.

"I got so tired I could barely keep my eyes open after staring at the books."

"You're sure that's all it is?"

Emily sat up. "What else could it be, Lucas?"

"Could you be pregnant?"

Emily laughed. "No. No chance of that."

He nodded. "Just tired then." He sighed.

She tilted her head. "Were you hoping I was pregnant?"

Lucas shrugged and grinned. "I want kids but I think we need to get rid of Adam first."

At the mention of Adam's name, Munch growled from her spot on the windowsill.

"Yes. Something you and I agree on, cat," Lucas muttered.

"What happened?"

Lucas stared at Emily. "He offered me ten million for you." At Emily's gasp, he continued. "I told him there wasn't enough money to hand you over and then I shoved him into his car and told him he'd better not come near you or he'd deal with me."

Emily got to her knees and hugged him. "Thank you."

"No need to thank me, darlin'. I'm not interested in his money. He also told me I'd get full ownership in Whispering Pines if you were out of the picture."

"I hate that man," she said.

"I feel the same way. He's showing his hand now. I'm sure he'll start getting more ballsy."

Chapter Six

Emily kissed his cheek and left the bed. Lucas followed her from the room and down the stairs. She stopped at the bottom and gazed back at him.

"I have to work on the sales sheets then I'll fix dinner." She headed down the hall to the office.

Once inside, she sat at the desk and covered her face with her hands. She knew Adam would offer Lucas money. She'd been surprised at the amount. Lucas turning it down made her feel wonderful but then, she knew he would. Money didn't matter to him. She lowered her hands and frowned. Why wouldn't it matter to him? He didn't grow up with money and with most people it would make them want it even more. Standing, she was about to go ask him when he filled the doorway.

"Why didn't you take the money?" she asked softly.

"What?" He frowned at her.

"You grew up without money, didn't you?"

Lucas moved into the room and took a seat in one of the wingback chairs. "Yes."

"Then why wouldn't you want ten million dollars?"

Lucas laughed. "Money isn't everything."

"It is to a lot of people, Lucas." Emily sat back down.

"I'm part owner in one of the best horse ranches in the states, it's all I want."

"Is that all?" She couldn't keep the hurt from her voice.

Lucas ran his hand along his jaw and sighed. "No. I want a family too." He stood and ambled around the desk and crouched down in front of her. "I want you."

Emily smiled through tears. "I want you too. I want a family with you, Lucas."

"Once we get rid of him, we're going to start on our family." He leaned forward and pressed his lips to hers. "I don't remember what my life was like before you Emily."

She wrapped her arms around his neck. "I think we need to go upstairs."

Lucas's eyebrows rose. "Didn't you just wake up?"

"Yes, but I didn't say we'd be sleeping."

Lucas laughed. "Now you're talking." He stood and pulled her to her feet then led her to the chair behind the desk and sat in the chair, pulling her onto his lap. "But I don't think we need to go upstairs." He lowered his mouth to her neck and nibbled.

Emily pulled away from him. "No?"

Lucas lifted her shirt over her head and groaned when he saw her black demi-cup bra. Looking into her eyes, he unhooked the clasp and then watched her breasts spill free. He leaned down and took a nipple into his mouth. Emily's fingers plowed through his hair, pulling him closer. He moved his mouth across her chest to the other one. Emily moaned and wrapped her arms around his head. She stood and removed her jeans and panties. Lucas groaned.

"God, you are so gorgeous," he said as he pulled her toward him and kissed her belly. She reached down, unsnapped his jeans, and slowly lowered the zipper. His hard shaft strained against his boxer briefs. He lifted up and shoved them down. Emily wrapped her hand around him. He closed his eyes.

"I need you now, darlin'."

"Yes," she whispered as she straddled him and slowly inched down over him. He clenched his jaw until she settled down over him. She gazed into his eyes then started to lift herself from him, then down over him again. Both of them moaned. His hands grasped her hips to set a rhythm. Her hands grasped his shoulders, her head going back. She ground against him and pressed her lips to his as her orgasm hit her, groaning into his mouth as she came. Lucas arched up into her then stood and laid her on the desk, with her legs around his waist, he pounded into her. His hands moved over her breasts as he watched her face flush. It threw him over the edge. He came hard but couldn't stop moving against her until he was spent. Leaning over, he kissed her with all the passion he felt.

"I'll never get enough of you," he said against her lips then took her bottom lip between his teeth and tugged on it.

"And I'll never get enough of you." She pulled him to her and kissed him, running her tongue into his mouth making him groan. She pulled back to look at him.

He was getting hard again. "This won't take long at all," he said, as he started moving against her fast and hard. She cried out his name just as he growled low in his chest.

She laughed. "That should be a record."

Lucas chuckled. "World's fastest fuck?"

She blushed at his crude language but laughed. "Yes, I would think so."

Lucas straightened up and helped her up. "I'll never be able to sit at this desk again without getting hard."

Emily swatted at him. "God! You can be so crude."

Lucas burst out laughing. "Just telling it like it is darlin'."

She put her clothes on and headed toward the door. As she walked away from him, she glanced over her shoulder at him and smiled. They had a good marriage and she just hoped it stayed that way.

* * * *

Lucas sat at the desk and smiled. Married life wasn't so bad. The sex was great. Emily was great. It was all great. So why did he feel it could be so much more? He leaned his head back and closed his eyes. Something had to be done about Walters and soon. Lucas wanted to get on with their lives. He heard the shower running and smiled thinking of her in there and his groin tightened. How the hell could he be aroused again?

Lucas sighed, stood, and headed out to the barn to get some work done. Stopping at his truck, he retrieved the salt bag and carried it into the barn. Tinker stood inside the door. Lucas set the bag down, took his knife out, and cut the bag open.

"Can you get the feed buckets? We'll mix this in with it."

"Sure," Tinker said as he moved toward the stalls. He came back carrying four buckets.

There were twenty-five horses on the ranch. Lucas scooped the salt and poured it into the oats. The horses needed the salt to keep minerals in their bodies. With summer coming, they would need more of it. After scooping salt into the buckets, Tinker took them away and came back with more. Once all the horses had salt, Lucas and Tinker headed into the back office and got a couple of beers out.

"I'll be glad when today's over," Tinker said.

"Something wrong?"

"My damn knees are killing me today. I'm supposed to have surgery but who has the time?"

Lucas sat forward in his chair. "Go get it done, Tinker. I can run things around here."

"I'd be out for a while. I can't afford it. I get paid well here but being off from work would catch up with me." Tinker shook his head.

Lucas nodded. "I understand, but you can't keep going like this. You'll get down and not get back up."

Tinker laughed. "I sure hope not but I ain't gettin' no younger."

"No you're not. Get the surgery, Tinker. We'll pay you while you're off."

Tinker's eyebrows shot up. "You can't do that."

Lucas laughed. "Why the hell not? I'm part owner and I can guarantee Emily will go along with it." He put his hand up when Tinker started to interrupt. "It's settled. Go call your doctor and make the appointment. That's an order."

Tinker's cheeks turned red. "I appreciate it Lucas, but—"

"No buts. Go home now and call your doctor." Lucas leaned back, clasped his hands across his flat stomach, and stared at Tinker.

Tinker sighed and stood. He put his hand out to Lucas. "I'm sorry I was a pain in the ass when you first got here. I was only thinking of Emily."

"I know. It's fine, we're good."

Tinker's eyes were suspiciously bright. "As long as you treat her good, I'm fine with it and to tell you the truth, I've never seen her happier." He pointed at Lucas. "And it's because of you." He left without another word.

Lucas smiled. He hoped Tinker was right and he did make Emily happy. God knew she made him happy. He needed to get some work done and then he would let Emily know about Tinker's operation. He sighed as he picked up the papers for the sale of five of the horses.

* * * *

Emily was in the kitchen when the phone rang. "Whispering Pines," she answered.

"Your new husband's an idiot."

Emily gasped. "Because he didn't take the money?"

Adam laughed and it grated on her nerves. "So he told you? I'm surprised."

"Lucas is honest with me. It's what a marriage is about. You wouldn't know about that."

"You bitch. You're going to regret divorcing me," he growled.

"The only thing I regret is marrying you to begin with. Don't threaten me. You don't scare me anymore." She tried desperately to keep the tremor out of her voice.

"Oh it's not a threat, you can bet your ass on that." Adam hung up.

She stood there with the receiver in her hand when Lucas came in. He rushed to her.

"What's wrong?"

"Adam..." she cleared her throat. "It was Adam. He said I'd regret divorcing him."

"Son of a bitch," Lucas roared as he headed toward the door.

Emily ran after him. "Where are you going?"

"To look for the bastard."

"No! Lucas, please. You can't do this." Tears rolled down her face. "Please. Don't go after him. I can't lose you."

Lucas blew out a breath and pulled her into his arms. "All right. I won't, but if he comes around here, I will not be responsible for my actions."

Emily clung to him and nodded. "Thank you."

Lucas squeezed her tighter. She couldn't stop the tears from coming on harder. It had to end soon. Someway, it had to end or she was going to lose her sanity.

* * * *

Lucas sat in the office alone and stared at the wall. Walters was out there making plans. No one had mentioned seeing him since he'd entered the bank and strutted around like he owned it. Lucas knew he was just biding his time. The thoughts were not good, of what Walters could do. He was ruthless in his pursuit of Emily and Lucas knew she was terrified.

Lucas sighed and stood. He moved toward the window and gazed out. The weather was getting nicer and the snow was melting fast. Maybe it was his plan. No footprints would show if the snow was gone. Lucas grunted. The man was smart. Emily had told Lucas he was. The son of a bitch was patient too.

"Hey," Emily said softly from the doorway.

Lucas turned to smile at her. She hadn't slept much in the past few days and it showed. He strode to her. "You look so tired. Why don't you try to get some sleep?"

She shook he head. "I can't sleep."

"I'm here with you, Emily. He won't get to you as long as I'm with you." He ran his hand over her hair. "You need to get some sleep, darlin'."

"Will you lie down with me?" She gazed up at him with those big green eyes.

"I'll stay with you until you fall asleep. I have work I need to get done."

She wrapped her arms around his waist. "We have ranch hands for that, Lucas."

He sighed. "All right. Let's go take a nap." He led her from the room and upstairs. They lay on the bed and Lucas held her to him as she put her head on his chest. Only minutes passed before he knew she was asleep. He rested his cheek on the top of her head and closed his eyes. He'd die before he'd let Walters take her from him.

* * * *

Emily woke up alone and quickly glanced around the room. The sun was still shining through the window. She stretched and headed downstairs to find Lucas in the kitchen, sitting at the table. His laptop sat in front of him. He glanced up when she entered.

"Hi. Do you feel rested?"

Emily nodded. "Yes. When did you leave the room?"

"Just a few minutes ago. I woke up and decided to get back with some of the emails we received about some horses. We have ten people interested in buying."

"That's good. We'll get some of the mares pregnant this spring and sell even more next year."

Lucas nodded and went back to the emails while she got herself a cup of tea. She took a seat beside him sipping her tea as he answered emails. They both jumped when Tinker burst through the back door without knocking.

"We have a horse down!" He ran back outside with Emily and Lucas running behind him. They entered the barn and moved to the stall where Star Gazer lay panting.

"Colic?" Lucas asked Tinker.

"I don't know. I called the vet. He'll be here any minute. I've tried getting Star up but he won't budge. If it is colic, we have to get him up before he rolls and twists his intestines."

Lucas ran from the stall then returned in a few minutes with a long, wide strap. All three of them worked together to get the strap under the horse and try to raise him up. Lucas called the ranch hands on his cell. A few minutes later, they came running into the barn to help. It was of no use, the horse would not stand. The vet, Doctor Tyler Woods, arrived and checked the horse for impaction or stomach rumbling. He shook his head when he took the stethoscope out of his ears.

"It's not colic. He's not impacted and his stomach doesn't seem to be bothering him. I'm going to draw some blood and test it."

Everyone stood back to let the doctor do what was needed. All of a sudden, the horse laid his head down. The vet kneeled down to check him. He glanced at Lucas. "He's still breathing but it's very shallow. I need to get some fluids into him. Now."

"No," Emily shouted as she kneeled down.

"I'm sorry Emily but he may not make it."

Emily sat back on her heels and stared at him. "He has to. Do something."

Doctor Woods gazed up at Lucas. "I'm doing all I can for him. I'm hoping the fluids will help him. He's a healthy horse. I don't understand what's going on."

Emily stood and clenched her hands into fists as tears rolled down her face. "Oh, I know what caused it or I should say who caused it." She shook her head. "Adam did this."

Lucas put his arm around her. "How? We've been watching for him. All of us have kept an eye out for him. There's no way he walked onto this ranch and did this."

Emily pushed him away. "He did! Apparently none of you are watching hard enough." She strode from the barn.

* * * *

Lucas sighed and turned to go after her when Tinker laid a hand on his arm. "Let her go, Lucas. She's upset and needs to be alone. She didn't mean what she said."

Lucas nodded. "He couldn't have done this, could he, Tinker? We're keeping an eye out." He glanced around at the other men and they all nodded.

"We're not even sure it was him, Lucas. Emily's freaked out right now. It could've been anything. A snake maybe." Tinker shrugged. "It could any number of things and until Doctor Woods finds out, we're just guessing."

"These fluids should help flush out any toxins," Doctor Woods told them.

Lucas shook his hand. "I appreciate it, Tyler. I'm going inside with Emily. What do you want us to do with Star Gazer?"

"I'm staying until I'm sure he's going to be all right." Doctor Woods sighed. "I'll do everything in my power to save him. She loves this horse. Her grandfather bought him almost twenty years ago and she grew up with him." He stared at Lucas. Lucas nodded as he left the barn and headed toward the house. Taking a deep breath, he entered the kitchen and took his hat and coat off. He ran his fingers through his hair and went in search of his wife. He found her in the living room, curled up in the window seat. Her cheeks were tearstained. He sat beside her but when he reached for her, she pulled away from him.

"You can't blame us for this."

She narrowed her eyes at him. "He walked on to this ranch, God knows when, and did something to my horse. No one saw him, but yet I can't blame any of you?"

"That's not fair Emily. We don't even know what's made him sick—"

She jumped up. "We *do* know! It was Adam, and if you don't believe it then you're a fool." She started to walk away when Lucas grasped her arm.

"I'll wait for the results from the vet before I jump to conclusions, and you should too. There's no way he walked on this ranch without being seen. You need to realize that."

"Maybe you took the money," she shouted.

"*What?* What did you just say to me?" Lucas clenched his teeth so hard they ached. "You can't be serious."

She shrugged. "It's funny how no one saw him."

"It might not have been him," Lucas roared.

"You'd love for me to believe that, wouldn't you?" She jerked her arm from him. "Get out and leave me alone."

"You want me to leave? You married me so I could protect you and now you're throwing me out? Who's going to protect you? An old man and one ranch hand here each night. Get real."

"I'll take care of myself." She moved further away from him.

"I'm not going anywhere. I own half of this ranch and whether you like it or not, I'm staying."

They glared at each other until Emily turned away from him. "I don't care what you do. I'm going upstairs to move my things back to my room."

Lucas watched her climb the stairs then he took a deep breath and followed her up. When she entered their bedroom, he closed the door and leaned back against the door. She glanced over to him.

"What do you think you're doing?" She put her hands on her hips and glared at him.

"Not letting my wife out of our bedroom."

"Lucas Taggart, you will not keep me in this room against my will."

Lucas grinned. "I don't think it will be against your will." He shoved himself away from the door and moved slowly toward her. She backed up until she hit the wall behind her. She shook her head. Lucas cupped her face in his hands and lowered his lips to hers.

"You seriously think I had something to do with it?" He pressed his lips to hers. When she moaned, he pulled her tightly against him and deepened the kiss. Raising his head slowly, he gazed into her eyes. "I swear I didn't."

A tear rolled down her cheek. "I know you didn't. I'm sorry." More tears followed.

Lucas lifted her in his arms and laid her on the bed. He held her while she cried. When she finally fell asleep, he went back to the barn to talk with Tinker.

"How long have the men worked here?" He asked Tinker.

Tinker seemed surprised by the question. "A good while."

Lucas sighed. "Okay, then do you know if any of them are having financial problems or if any of them would take money?"

"You mean to harm Star Gazer?" At Lucas's nod, Tinker went on. "I would hope none of them."

"Damn it, Tinker, I hope the same, but if that horse was poisoned, someone on this ranch may have played a part in it."

Tinker ran his hand down his face. "I don't know who would do it. They love the horses here too. I can't see any of them doing this, even for money."

"Walters couldn't have gotten on this ranch. You've been rotating the men so we have one here every night, right?"

"Yep. I'll talk to them." Tinker strolled away.

Lucas headed back to the house. When he entered the kitchen, Emily was sitting at the table. She wouldn't look up at him. He moved to squat down in front of her.

"Hey," he said softly. She raised her eyes to his. He could see she was still crying and lifted a hand to brush her tears away. "I'm so sorry about Star Gazer, baby."

Emily nodded. "I'm sorry I accused you. I was hurt. I know you would never hurt any animal, especially a horse. You love them as much as I do."

"It's all right, I knew you were upset. We'll get to the bottom of this. Tinker's going to talk with the men. I hate to think it could be one of them but we have to look at everyone."

"I know. Those men have worked here for as long as I can remember, I just can't see them doing anything like that."

Lucas stood and put his hand out to her. "We've had a rough day and we still need to get Star Gazer better. Do you want to go back to the barn with me?"

"Yes," she said softly.

Lucas gave a terse nod and they walked outside together. Tinker was heading toward them.

"What is it now?" Lucas asked warily.

"Nick says he was on watch last night." Tinker glanced away and then back to them. "He said he woke up on the floor around three in the morning. Swears he didn't fall asleep though."

"He didn't think to tell us?" Lucas was angry.

"He was scared but he swears he didn't fall sleep. He said he was sitting in the chair in the barn and the next thing he knew, he woke up on the floor."

"Get him and bring him to the house. Now." Lucas and Emily walked back inside to wait for them. When Nick and Tinker walked in, Lucas motioned for them to sit. He glared at Nick.

"How could you not tell us about this, Nick?" Emily asked.

"I was afraid you would accuse me of harming Star Gazer." He swallowed. "I would never hurt any animal. Star Gazer is one of my favorites. I swear Miz Emily, I didn't hurt him."

"Tell us what happened," Lucas demanded.

Nick shrugged. "Just like I told Tinker. I was sitting in the chair and the next thing I know, I'm on the floor waking up around three."

"You weren't knocked out?" Emily asked softly.

"No Miz Emily. I don't have a lump on my head and it doesn't hurt anywhere." Nick glanced at Lucas. "I swear Mister Taggart, I didn't hurt Star Gazer."

Lucas stood and paced. "Well, something happened to him. A horse as healthy as he is doesn't just up and get so sick he can't stand for no God damn reason. You were the last one with him."

"Lucas..." Emily pleaded.

"No." Lucas put his hand up. "This needs to be done. I want to know what happened last night." He turned to Nick. "Did you see anyone? Was anyone here?"

"No. I didn't—" Nick stopped.

"What?" Lucas pulled a chair out, spun it around, and straddled it.

"The only person here was Marylou Johnson. She brought me some coffee."

"In a cup of some kind?" Tinker asked.

Nick nodded. "Yes. She just showed up. I was surprised to see her but she's real pretty so I didn't question it." He hung his head. "I suppose I should have."

"Where's the cup?"

"I guess still in the barn. I forgot about it."

Lucas stood and ran out the door. A few minutes later, he came back in with the cup and called the sheriff, Nathan Walker. He told Lucas he'd be right there.

"Am I going to lose my job?" Nick asked, gazing at Emily. She glanced at Lucas.

"It depends on what we find, but I have a feeling someone gave Marylou money to drug you enough to make you pass out. If that's the case, no, you won't lose your job but no one is allowed on this property unless Emily and I are asked. We clear?" Lucas stared at him.

"Yes sir." Nick hung his head.

Emily stood and got him a glass of water. His hands shook as he took the glass from her. Lucas moved toward the coffee pot to make some. Emily sat down beside Nick and put her hand over his. Tinker sighed and sat down with them. They waited for the sheriff to show up.

After the sheriff questioned Nick, he took the cup, said he'd talk with Marylou and left. Lucas told Nick he was to take some days off until the investigation was over. Nick wasn't happy about it but he understood and left. Tinker started out the door when Lucas stopped him.

"Set up a schedule so we can all take turns watching Star."

Tinker nodded and glanced at Emily. "You don't need to go back out there."

"Yes I do," she whispered.

Tinker gave a nod and walked out with Lucas and Emily behind him. Lucas took her hand in his and squeezed it. She squeezed back as they headed toward the barn.

Chapter Seven

Adam watched through binoculars from his spot in the north pasture. He laughed when he saw them all heading for the barn. He'd been in the pasture the entire time the sheriff was there. Marylou did a marvelous job last night and hopefully the ranch hand wouldn't remember her being there. There'd been enough Xanax in the cup to knock an elephant out. He stood and made his way down the hill to the dirt road running along the property. It was easy to slip into the pasture from the road. It didn't seem as if it'd been used very often. Getting into his car, he pulled out and headed back to the motel.

When he stepped from the car, he saw the woman he'd paid to drug the ranch hand standing by his door. He sighed and strolled toward her. "What are you doing here? We can't take a chance on being seen together."

"I want the rest of my money now."

"You'll get the rest in a few days." Adam curbed his temper.

"I can go to the sheriff," Marylou told him.

He sneered. "I'll take you down with me. Now get the hell out of here. I'll contact you in a few days as we agreed."

She sighed and left. Adam entered the room and took a shower. It wouldn't be long now. He'd have Emily again. They were going to go away together. If she didn't want to go he'd make her or kill her. He shrugged. It didn't really matter to him. With his looks, he had no trouble attracting women. The stupid bitches.

Adam laid on the bed, clasped his hands behind his head, and stared up at the ceiling. It was going to taste so sweet when he got Emily back. He couldn't wait to have her under him again and he would, there was no doubt in his mind. She couldn't resist him anymore than any other woman could. He smiled as he fell asleep

* * * *

As Emily stood watching Star Gazer lying in his stall, she shivered. The horse had been a family member for almost as long as she was alive. She could remember sitting on the horse with her grandfather while he rode the fences in the pastures. The tears rolled down her face as she clung to Lucas's hand and watched Star Gazer's labored breathing. Tinker came in to relieve them. Emily couldn't take anymore and ran toward the house. She had to get away from everyone for a while. Once inside she ran upstairs and into the bedroom then threw herself across the bed. Sobs wracked her body, but she couldn't seem to stop them. She felt Lucas touch her back. She rolled over, and gazed up at him. Tears made it difficult to see. He pulled her into his arms and held her tightly.

"I'm so sorry, Emily. So very sorry," he murmured as he rubbed her back.

"I hate him. I know he poisoned my horse. He's cruel enough to do it."

"I'm sure we'll hear from Doctor Woods in a day or two. He took a blood sample with him. If Star Gazer was poisoned, then it had to be Walters. No one on this ranch would harm any of those animals." He kissed her forehead. "We'll just wait a few days."

Emily nodded. "All right but I know he did something to Star. I know it, Lucas."

Lucas held her and murmured to her. It was going to take her a while to get over this.

* * * *

Two days later, Lucas and Emily drove Tinker to the hospital for his surgery. They would wait during the operation and then drive him home. A woman from town was coming to look after him.

"I appreciate you two doing this for me," Tinker said from the backseat.

"Would you just shut the hell up about it?" Lucas muttered.

Tinker laughed. "The man can't accept any appreciation."

Emily laughed. "I think you're right, Tinker." She reached for Tinker's hand. "We love you, we're family."

Tinker didn't say more. They pulled into the parking lot of the hospital and walked inside. Once the nurse took Tinker back for surgery, Emily and Lucas sat in the waiting room. She took his hand in hers.

"We have a lot of time to wait. Tell me about your childhood. You've put it off long enough."

Lucas growled and sighed. "Shit. I was hoping you forgot."

Emily laughed softly. "Nope. Now spill it."

Lucas ran his hands down his face, leaned forward, and rested his elbows on his knees.

"My dad left before I was born. I never knew him. I'm not blaming him for my wild ways, that was all me. My mom didn't know what to do with me from the time I was twelve until I was in my teens. I ran with a rough group. All of us were from broken homes but that was no excuse for the shit we did. I was fourteen when I stole my first car." He shook his head. "I didn't get caught so I did it again. I was boosting my third car when I did get caught. I was lying in the car, under the steering wheel with my feet out of the car, when I felt someone kick my foot. I glanced up and saw this big man standing over me. He says, 'go ahead, I want to see if you can do it.' I tried to get out and run but he had me by my shirt collar before I even got out of the car." Lucas chuckled. "I'd tried to steal a car belonging to a cop. Bill took me into his house, sat me on the couch, and stared at me. I glared at him and told him he didn't scare me. He laughed and said 'yes I do.' He was right. I was scared to death I'd go to Juvie. The prick made me call my mom. To say she was pissed would be a huge understatement. When she got there, I was sure she was going to kill me. Bill told her he wouldn't press charges if I agreed to clean up my act. Of course, I stood up and yelled 'fuck you', which had my mom slapping me for the first time ever. She looked as shocked as I felt. I agreed to do as he asked because I hated hurting my mom. Once I started doing better in school, the other guys I ran with did too. We all graduated top of the class. But we always had the wild reputation. It will always be there. Many people still look down on us although we've all done well for ourselves. I have more than enough money to buy Whispering Pines five times over." He shrugged. "It doesn't matter, though. We'll always be the bad boys of Dry River." He glanced over to her. "So, you married a car thief. You want to divorce me?"

Emily smiled at him. "No way are you getting out of this marriage. I don't care about your past, Lucas. Just our future." She shook her head. "I can't believe you have that kind of money. Why didn't you tell me?"

Lucas glanced away then back to her. "I didn't think it mattered. I put it in the Whispering Pines bank account. It's our money, just like Whispering Pines is ours. Together. Isn't that what married couples do?"

"Yes it is, but it's your money."

"No. It's *ours.* It's there for our future. Our children's futures. College or whatever they want to do."

Emily leaned her head on his shoulder. "Thank you," she whispered. "Wait. Bill? Isn't that the name of your mom's new husband?"

Lucas chuckled. "One and the same. He wanted to marry her years ago but she was afraid of getting hurt." He shrugged. "Bill finally convinced her, and I love him like a dad."

"It certainly turned out well for all of you, didn't it?" Emily smiled. "Why did you leave here five years ago?"

Lucas shrugged. "I got restless."

"Let's hope you don't again."

Lucas nodded and put his arm around her while they waited for word about the surgery.

The doctor came into the waiting room a few hours later to let them know Tinker was fine and the surgery went well. He could go home in a few hours if he was still doing well. Lucas and Emily left to go to dinner. They would be back to take him home later. They walked out of the hospital hand in hand then drove to the diner to enjoy dinner together.

A few days later, Doctor Woods called and told them Star Gazer had Foxglove in his blood but luckily not enough to kill him. He advised them to empty the food buckets and put fresh food in. Star Gazer would survive. Emily knew Adam was behind it, she just couldn't prove it. Marylou left town and no one seemed to know where she'd gone. Emily wouldn't be surprised if Adam was behind that too. She knew he was an evil man. He may not have killed Marylou but she wouldn't put it past him to hire someone to do it.

* * * *

May brought warmer weather. Adam hadn't called again and no one had seen him. Emily knew he was still out there. Plotting. Tinker healed up and worked about the ranch much easier. She was happy to have him back and she knew Lucas was too. She decided to go out to visit them. It was such a beautiful day, a horseback ride sounded perfect. Of course, Lucas would have to go with her and she knew he'd only go if he wasn't busy. She smiled as she crossed the yard and entered the barn. Letting her eyes adjust, she stood inside the door.

Lucas sauntered toward her smiling. "Hey darlin'. What are you doing out here?"

"It's so pretty out. I thought we could go for a horseback ride. I can pack a picnic."

Lucas grinned. "Can we make love in the pasture?" He chuckled when she blushed. "Is that a yes?"

Emily blushed and nodded. "Of course."

Lucas kissed her and pulled her tight against him. "I'll saddle the horses. You go make a lunch for us."

Emily smiled up at him. "All right."

They both jumped when they heard an explosion. Lucas grabbed her arms. "Stay here." He ran from the barn. Tinker and the other ranch hands came running from different directions.

* * * *

Lucas halted in his tracks when he saw his pick-up truck on fire.

"Call 9-1-1," he shouted as he ran for the hose, but Lucas knew it was a lost cause as he turned to see the flames reaching for the sky. The truck was a total loss. He glanced toward the barn then ran for it. Once inside, he gazed around but didn't see Emily anywhere.

"Emily," he shouted as he ran through the barn.

Tinker entered. "Maybe she went in the house."

Lucas shook his head. "She wouldn't do that without telling me," he shouted for her again.

"She's gotta be here," Tinker yelled as he ran outside. Lucas followed him to the house. They both ran inside and shouted. No answer. Lucas had a bad feeling.

"He has her," he whispered.

"No," Tinker said. "We would've seen him."

"We were too interested in the truck. It was a diversion and it worked." Lucas paced. *"Son of a bitch!"* Lucas picked up a glass and threw it against the wall. He spun around to look at Tinker. "I will kill him if he hurts her."

Tinker nodded. They heard the sirens at the same time and walked outside. The fire truck pulled up with the Sheriff's cruiser behind it. Lucas strode toward the sheriff.

"We think Emily's been taken by her ex-husband Adam Walters."

Sheriff Walker stopped in his tracks. "Kidnapping?"

Lucas nodded. "He took her from right under our noses. He somehow had the truck explode and grabbed her when we ran toward it." Lucas glanced away then back to him. "He'll hurt her Nathan. He wants revenge." Lucas swore. "I shouldn't have left her in the barn. When we heard the explosion, I should have grabbed her and kept her with me. I should have known it was him."

"Don't blame yourself, Lucas. I have to call the FBI for a kidnapping. I'll help them as much as I can but something like this is their field." Nathan took his cell phone from his pocket. "I'll call Mont. He'd want to be in on this since you're friends." Nathan spoke into the phone, hung up and turned to Lucas. "He's on his way."

Lucas headed for the front porch steps and sat down. He ran his hands over his head. Nathan stepped in front of him.

"We'll find her, Lucas," he murmured.

Lucas raised his head. "I hope you do before he kills her."

"You know Mont will do all he can to find her in time." Nathan sat down beside him. "I'll have the truck taken in to see how it exploded. My guess is someone shot the gas tank from a good distance away and Walters was close enough by to grab Emily and take her without any of you seeing them."

"We all ran toward the truck. I told her to stay in the barn." Lucas ran his hands down his face. "I shouldn't have left her alone."

"Anyone would have done the same thing, Lucas. It was instinct for you to run toward the explosion and think Emily would be safe in the barn."

"If he hurts her, he's a dead man."

"I'll pretend I didn't hear that." Nathan stood and stared down at him. "I'll get my deputies out looking and since Dakota's in town, I'll have him round up your friends and they can look too."

"All right. I'd appreciate it, Nathan." Lucas stood and entered the house. He wanted to be alone until Mont arrived.

* * * *

Emily woke up groggy and gazed around but didn't recognize where she was. It was dark and dank. The smell was musty. Her hands were behind her back, tied together, as were her ankles. Adam. It had to be him. She didn't remember seeing him. The last thing she remembered was the explosion and Lucas telling her to stay put. Adam must have grabbed her then. He must have set something to explode to get everyone to run toward it so he could take her. She blinked the tears from her eyes. He was going to kill her. She knew it. He hated her for divorcing him. The thought of dying before she had a chance to tell Lucas she loved him made her heart ache. He'd never know her entire world revolved around him. She choked back a sob when she heard footsteps and scooched back against a wall. A pair of Italian leather shoes stopped in front of her. Her eyes ran up a pair of black dress pants to a white shirt then to the face of the man she hated most in life.

"Adam," she said through clenched teeth.

"You were expecting someone else?" He laughed as he squatted down in front of her. "I've been waiting for this."

"If you're going to kill me, just do it and get it over with."

Adam laughed. "Oh no. I want your *husband* to find you first. That way, I can kill you both."

"Leave Lucas out of this. He has nothing to do with what's between us."

"He's your husband. You divorced me to marry him."

Emily shook her head. "No. I asked him to marry me to protect me from you."

"That's rich. He didn't do a very good job of it did he? I have you now."

"Adam, please. Don't hurt him. You and I can go away together." Emily wanted to throw up even suggesting such a thing.

"I'm not stupid, Emily. I know you don't mean it. You're just trying to get me to leave him alone."

She scooted up to her knees. "No. I do mean it. We'll go away together. We can go anywhere you want."

He leaned down and put his face close to hers. "I'm not going anywhere with you. After I take care of both of you, I'm heading north into Canada. They'll never find me." He straightened up, "They'll never find you either." With that, he spun on his heel and started toward the stairs.

"You always were a cruel man. You poisoned my horse, didn't you?"

Adam burst out laughing. "Yes. I put Foxglove in his feed after your ranch hand passed out." He turned to face her.

"Did you pay Marylou to knock Nick out?"

"It's amazing what people will do for money. Except your husband. If he'd taken the money, we wouldn't be having this conversation. You and I could be in Canada enjoying our new life." He shook his head. "No. I'm done with you. It'll be over soon."

"What about Marylou? Where is she now?"

Adam laughed. "What makes you think I know or care?" He spun on his heel and headed upstairs.

The tears rolled down her cheeks. She knew it would do no good to shout. Since Adam hadn't covered her mouth, she knew they had to be somewhere no one would find her. She laid down on the floor and cried. Cried for herself and Lucas. What was he thinking right now? She knew without a doubt he'd look for her but she was so frightened of Adam getting to him. Lucas didn't deserve to die for any of this. Emily had been the one to ask him to marry her to protect her, and now he was in danger. *Damn you Adam! Damn you!*

* * * *

Lucas paced in the living room. This staying around and doing nothing wasn't sitting well with him. He needed to be out there, looking for Emily. His wife. He flopped down on the sofa and leaned his head back. Closing his eyes, he thought of how much he wanted her back. How much he loved her. How he wanted to tell her.

Putting the heels of his hands on his eyes, he rubbed them. They were gritty. He hadn't slept since Emily had been taken three days ago. When was Adam going to make his move? Tilting his head back, he let out a sigh. Munch jumped onto the sofa and meowed at him. Lucas stared at the cat.

"Yeah, I know. I miss her too cat."

"We'll do what we can Lucas."

Lucas turned his head to see his friend Montgomery Bradford standing by the sofa.

"I have no doubt you'll find her, Mont, but will it be soon enough?"

Mont took a seat in the chair opposite him. "There really isn't a lot we can do until he makes a move."

"It could be too late by then." Lucas jumped up and glared at his friend.

"He has an agenda. He'll call you or have Emily call you but he'll get in touch then we'll find him."

Lucas strode over to him. "What if you don't? He has revenge on his mind for her moving on without him." Lucas clenched his hands into fists.

Mont stood slowly. "I'm sure you're right, but he wants to make you suffer too. Trust me on this. I know what I'm talking about here."

The two men glared at each other until Lucas gave a terse nod. "We have to find her, Mont."

"There is no 'we' Lucas. You will leave this to the FBI. Believe it or not, we know what we're doing."

"Shit, I know. It's just that it's been three days. He has a head start on you."

"He hasn't called yet. He will," Mont said with certainty.

"I don't know why he'd call, Mont. The man doesn't need money. He's loaded."

"He has an agenda, I'm telling you. He took her for a reason and since you *politely* put him in his car, he's going to enjoy making you wait."

Lucas swore and sat down. He laid his arms on his knees and his hands on his head. The sitting and waiting was slowly killing him. What was Walters waiting on? Lucas quickly stood and strode from the living room. Montgomery followed him.

"Don't even think of leaving."

"I have to get out of this house. I can't stand sitting here and waiting."

Mont grasped Lucas's arm. "You have to stay here in case he calls."

Lucas muttered under his breath and took a seat at the kitchen table. He glanced around and saw how empty the house seemed without Emily there. God! He missed her.

Mont sat down in a chair beside him. "I know you're worried but we have to let him get in touch with you. He can't do it if you're not here."

"He could call my cell phone, Mont." Lucas narrowed his eyes at his friend.

"Which you will put on speaker if he does. I need to listen to him. I need to be able to locate the son of a bitch in order to get to Emily." Mont shook his head. "I've been doing this for years now, Lucas. Let me handle it."

Lucas huffed and nodded. "All right, Mont. I'll listen to you."

Mont burst out laughing. "That's a first. Didn't I tell you not to steal that last car?"

"Fuck you Bradford," Lucas growled.

"That's *Agent* Bradford to you."

Lucas laughed for the first time in days. But he quickly sobered and stared at Mont. "I can't lose her, Mont."

"I know, Lucas. I can see how much you love her. I'll do what I can to get her back to you safe and sound."

The back door opened and Tinker came in with Storm, Cooper, Dakota, and Lincoln on his heels.

"We're here to do whatever you need, Lucas," Dakota told him.

"I appreciate it, but according to secret agent man here, there isn't anything to do until the bastard calls."

Mont smiled at Dakota and shrugged. "He's not real happy with me right now."

The men all took seats around the table and waited. Lucas paced while they played poker. When night fell and there was still no word, his friends left but told him to call if he needed them. Mont assured them he would.

* * * *

Emily sat in the dark basement listening to the voices upstairs. One was Adam but she had no idea who the others belonged to. She couldn't make out what they were saying, though. Glancing around, she tried to figure out a way to get away and the results were the same as the last four days. No windows or doors. Only the stairwell in front of her. Adam had untied her hands and showed her a bathroom to use in the basement. She shuddered. It looked as if it hadn't been cleaned in a decade.

The door at the top of the stairs opened, the light bulb above her came on, and she could hear several footsteps coming down. Emily scooted back to the corner. Three shadows loomed in front of her. She recognized Adam but the other two were strangers.

"Well, well, well. Look what we have here," one of them said.

Adam glared at him. "Back the fuck off. She's my wife."

The other man laughed. "She ain't your wife. She divorced your ass while you were in prison. I'd like a shot at that."

Adam grabbed the man by the collar and pulled him close. "You will not touch her. Do I make myself clear?" he said through clenched teeth.

The man nodded. "Yes. Jesus, Walters. I was just kidding."

Adam shoved him back. "That isn't something to kid about. Don't even look at her. Either of you."

The man who hadn't said anything just nodded. The other one straightened his shirt. Adam squatted down in front of Emily and reached a hand toward her. She jerked back. He glared at her.

"You should be nice to me," he whispered.

"Never. You make me sick," Emily shouted.

The men laughed until Adam spun around and stared at them. "Go upstairs. We're going to make a phone call in a few minutes." He turned to Emily. "Give me his number."

She shook her head. "No."

Adam sighed and stood. "I'll just call the house then, but if he has the police or FBI there and I find out, I'll make him suffer before I kill him."

"Adam, please—" She wasn't ready for the slap.

"Do not plead with me for him. Give me his number. Now." He grabbed her hair and pulled her face close to his.

Tears filled her eyes as she rattled it off to him and watched as he entered it into his phone then he left. She sat in the corner as the tears rolled down her face. How was she going to get out of this? If she could get away from Adam in some way, she could make her way back to Lucas. That's all she wanted to do, get back to Lucas and tell him she loved him.

* * * *

Lucas jerked when his cell phone rang. Mont ran into the living room with a raised hand.

"Wait. Put the phone on the table and on speaker." He nodded for Lucas to set the phone down.

Lucas sighed. "Hello?"

"No one else better be listening," Adam told him.

Lucas glanced at Mont. "I'm alone. Let me speak to Emily."

Adam laughed. "No. You and I are going to talk."

"I'm not saying anything to you until I know my wife is still alive."

"First, let's get something straight. She will *never* be your wife. It doesn't matter if you have a piece of paper stating otherwise. Emily belongs to me and she always will. Second, I don't have to prove anything to you, but I'll let you hear her. Just so you and I can come to an understanding."

Lucas could hear shuffling noises then Adam telling Emily to say something. Lucas was relieved when he heard Emily telling Adam to go to hell. He glanced up at Mont who nodded.

"She refuses to talk. You must have pissed her off." Adam's sinister laugh came across the line.

Lucas snorted. "You're an idiot. She's not talking because she doesn't want to upset me." Lucas looked at Mont and saw him glaring. Lucas shrugged. "All right. I know she's still alive. What do you want?"

"I want you Taggart. You and me. Alone."

Lucas grunted. "Now why don't I believe that? You already know I can kick your ass, so how do I know you'd come alone?"

Adam laughed. "You don't, but if you want to see Emily again, you'll show up. There's an abandoned house east of Whispering Pines on Carter's Bend. One hour." He ended the call.

Lucas glanced up at Mont. "I don't suppose you'd let me go alone."

Mont grumbled. "You know better."

Lucas sighed. "Then how are we doing this?"

"Let me think. I doubt if she's where he wants to meet, but we can't take any chances. If she is, we have to figure out a way to get in without being seen." Mont turned to the other two FBI agents in the room. "Get me a satellite view of the house."

"If he kills her, he's a dead man," Lucas told him.

"Don't make me arrest you, Lucas."

"I won't care if he kills her," Lucas said softly.

Mont stared at him before he spun on his heel and left the house. Lucas watched his friend go outside to the Sport Utility Vehicle, retrieve a laptop from it then came back in. He set it on the table then took a seat.

"The men will send me the map of the property in just a few minutes. Then we'll see what we can do." Mont stared at Lucas. "Do you know the property Walters is talking about?"

"If I'm right, it's the old Browne place."

Mont leaned back and folded his arms across his chest. "I remember the place. We used to sneak some girls into the barn."

Lucas laughed. "Yes, that's the place." He shook his head. "We were a rough bunch, Mont. All of us."

"Yep, we sure were." Mont chuckled. The computer screen lit up with a map of the property. Both men sat forward to gaze at the screen.

"The house doesn't look too bad but the land is a mess," Lucas said.

"That's good. We can sneak in. You drive in and I'll go through this field." Mont pointed at the screen. "I'll see if I can find her while you talk with Walters. Get him outside. Tell him you have no intention of going into the house with him. I'll get in and look for her and take out anyone else in there."

Lucas nodded. "All right. Just get her out if she's there."

"I will. I can promise you he isn't there alone though. He just wants you there so he can kill you and either kill her or take off with her."

"I know. There's no way I'm going to let him do any of that." Lucas looked at him. "You let me know if she's not in there. I'll get it out of him."

"Not going to happen, Lucas. If she isn't there, I'm taking him in."

"And just how do we find her then?"

"He'll want a deal. He has no desire to go back to prison."

Lucas glared at him. "You can't be serious?"

"Hell no, I'm not serious, but he won't know that."

Lucas nodded. "Good. He doesn't need any deal." He looked up when the other two agents strolled in.

"We'll get out of here in a few minutes." Mont glanced at the agents and nodded for them to go out. "I'm riding with you," he told Lucas.

"You don't trust me?"

"Not for a fucking second. You'll take out of here like a bat out of hell. We'll get him, Lucas. Agents Tucker and McCann will follow us."

Lucas sighed and nodded. He *had* planned to take off and lose them but with Mont going with him, it wasn't going to go his way. He ran his hand around the back of his neck. "All right. How are we handling this?"

"You're going to drop me off at the end of the road. I'll get to the house. Take your time getting to the house. I want to get into position before you even get close to the bastard."

"What about the other agents?"

"They'll park at the road and go in the opposite field. They'll be keeping an eye on you."

"You can't go into the house alone, Mont."

"Don't worry about me, you just keep Walters occupied. I have a silencer on my gun so I'll have to get the jump on anyone inside."

Lucas didn't like the odds. He was sure Walters had other men with him. He just wasn't sure how many he had and where they'd be. Mont was a good friend and he didn't want him hurt, but he was also a highly trained FBI agent.

"Let's do this," Lucas said as he headed toward the door.

"You need to calm the hell down first," Mont told him. "Unless you do, you will be staying behind."

"I can't stay behind. He wants me," Lucas growled.

"You're exactly right. So calm the hell down. You're not going in there guns blazing."

Lucas took a deep breath and blew it out. "I'm not. I just want to get this over with and get my wife home."

Mont nodded. "I understand, but I also know you and you're chomping at the bit to get there. I'm telling you if you go in there hell bent on beating the shit out of him, you'll get her killed. He'll see you coming from a mile away." Mont sighed. "Would you please just listen to me? I know what I'm doing."

Lucas stared at his friend for a few seconds before nodding. "All right. We'll do this your way but I'm telling you if he's killed her, I'll take him down."

"And I'll take you in. As much as I'd love to see him taken down, we have to do this legally. You will do what I say or you stay here. You understand me, Lucas?"

"Yes." Lucas clenched his jaw.

Mont gave a terse nod. "Good. Now, we'll go and you will do as I say or I'll make you turn the truck around and bring you back here."

They were about to go out the door when Tinker stepped onto the porch. He held his hat in his hand, his face lined with worry.

"You bring my girl home, Lucas."

"I will, Tinker." Lucas put his hand on Tinker's shoulder as he strode past him to the truck outside.

Chapter Eight

Emily jumped when the door at the top of the stairs opened and footsteps came down them and toward her. Adam stood in front of her with a smirk on his face. She glared up at him. He squatted down.

"Taggart is on his way here."

She gasped. "No. I don't believe you."

Adam laughed. "It doesn't matter if you do or not. You heard the conversation."

"Please, Adam. I'll go away with you."

"He'd come after us." He shook his head. "No. I need to get him out of the picture then I'll take care of you." He sighed. "I really can't make up my mind on what to do with you, Emily."

"If you hurt him, I won't go anywhere with you," she screamed at him.

"Then I'll just kill you both." He leaned down, put duct tape over her mouth, and then tied her hands behind her back. He spun on his heel and headed toward the stairs then turned back to her. "He should be here any time."

Emily tried to scream behind the tape but she knew it would do no good. Although he hadn't bound her legs, she knew she couldn't go anywhere. The only way out was the door at the top of the stairs and Adam and his two cohorts were there. Tears of frustration fell from her eyes. God, please don't let Lucas come here alone, but she knew he would. He'd come alone to take on Adam, if for no other reason. She didn't pray often but she did now.

* * * *

Lucas stopped the truck and watched as Mont got out then turned to him.

"Go slow so I can get through the field. McCann and Tucker will head through the other field. They'll be watching you in case anything goes wrong." Mont narrowed his eyes at him. "Don't get cocky. If something does go wrong, yell for them. They'll be there for you. I'm going into the house to look for Emily." He closed the door of the truck and headed toward the field.

"Mont," Lucas called after him. Mont turned around. "Be careful."

Mont gave a terse nod. "You too." Then he ran off.

Lucas sighed and drove the truck slowly down the road toward the house. He glanced to the left to look for Mont but he couldn't see him, then he glanced to the right but didn't see the other agents either. Lucas knew they were out there, but this was dangerous for all of them and he prayed Mont found Emily. Alive.

When he pulled up to the house, he turned the truck off and glanced around. He didn't see anyone but it didn't mean they weren't there and aiming at him. Opening the truck door, he slowly got out, leaned against the front fender of the truck, and waited for Walters to appear. Lucas clenched his fists. He wanted a shot at the asshole. He straightened up when the door to the house opened and Walters strolled out onto the porch. He stared at Lucas then smirked.

"You better be alone," Adam told him.

"Are you?" Lucas countered.

"I have two men in the house who are to kill Emily if you kill me."

"How do I know she's still alive?"

Adam laughed. "You don't. But you won't kill me if you know there's a chance she's still alive."

Lucas clenched his jaw. Son of a bitch. Mont needed to get into the house and find her. "So, what are we going to do? You know I'd like nothing better than to kill you."

"I feel the same about you. I want you out of her life. You agree to leave her with me and I'll let you live."

Lucas burst out laughing. "You'll *let* me live?" He quickly sobered. "Go to hell. I will not hand my wife over to you."

"You don't have a choice, Taggart. You're going to lose her either way. She goes with me, you live. You don't let her go, you die." Adam shrugged. "Simple."

Lucas swore. "There's nothing simple about it. One of us is going to die and it isn't going to be me." He took a step forward but halted when Adam pulled out a gun and aimed it at him as he moved down the steps of the porch.

"I thought we would settle this man to man, Walters." Lucas kept his eyes on Adam's face.

Adam laughed. "This isn't a pissing contest, Taggart. I'm going to kill you and then I'll decide what to do with Emily." He raised the gun, aimed and shot. Lucas fell to the ground.

* * * *

Emily heard the door to the basement open and then she saw two pairs of shoes coming down the stairs. She scooched back when she saw Adam's two men smiling at her.

"I think we're going to have a little fun with you since Walters is outside with your husband," one of them said to her. The other one laughed as he removed the tape over her mouth.

"I heard a gunshot," Emily said.

The men stopped and glanced at each other. "I didn't hear anything," one of them said. "Doesn't matter if you did or not. Whoever is standing, we plan on killing. We hate Walters but the money he offered was too good to turn down."

"I heard it when you were coming down the stairs."

The men laughed. "Nice try." They moved toward her.

Emily was terrified as she tried to get to her feet to run. The bigger man caught her and held her while the other tried to rip her shirt. She kicked out and got him in the groin and he fell down. The man holding her laughed. She screamed, all the while knowing it wouldn't help. All of a sudden, the man stilled and she heard another male voice.

"Let go of her and move against the wall or I'll blow your fucking head off."

"Who the fuck are you?" The man dropped Emily to the floor.

"FBI Agent Montgomery Bradford. Now move to the wall."

The man moved toward the wall. The man on the floor glared up at Mont. He started to stand. Emily saw Mont grin.

"Try it," he said in a low tone then nodded when the man stayed down. Mont glanced over to Emily. "Are you all right?" She nodded. "I'll be with you in a minute." He pulled out two pairs of handcuffs and secured the men then he strode toward her and helped her up.

"Lucas…"

"We'll check on him in a minute. I heard a shot but my men have silencers. I'll get you out of here and we'll see what happened."

"Are you saying something's wrong? If your men have silencers, who shot?" Emily frowned.

Mont shook his head. "I don't know. I couldn't take a chance using the radio in case one of these idiots heard me. Come on."

Emily nodded. She was sure she was going into shock when she started to shake.

Mont helped her up the stairs. She ran outside to see Lucas lying on the ground with two men squatting beside him, and Adam lying a few feet away. She ran to Lucas and kneeled down beside him.

"Lucas…please. No."

Lucas gazed up at her. "I'm all right, just stunned."

"Aren't you glad I made you wear the vest now?" Mont asked.

Lucas nodded. "Yes, but it still hurts like a bitch."

Mont chuckled. "Yeah, I know. Been there."

Lucas stood and pulled Emily to him and held her tight. "Are you all right?"

"I..I just want to go home," she whispered.

"Did you call an ambulance for Walters?" Mont asked McCann and Tucker.

"Yes, but if he dies before it gets here, it's no big loss," McCann said.

"I agree, but you know we have to get him to a hospital. Get an agent to keep guard on him, too. One of you needs to go downstairs to get the other two men." He turned toward Lucas. "I'll be over tomorrow to ask her questions. I should do it now but she's too upset and I doubt I'll get anything out of her."

She felt Lucas nod his head as he tightened his arms around her. Emily wanted to forget all of it but she knew she had to let the FBI know what happened. She pulled back from Lucas to gaze at the agents. "If you want to go back to Whispering Pines now, I'll be more than happy to tell you."

"Are you sure? I would like to talk with you about it."

"I'm positive. I'd like to get it out of the way." She shivered against Lucas.

"You don't have to do this now, Emily," Lucas told her.

"I want to. Please."

Lucas sighed. "All right. I'll take her home. We'll see you in a little while."

"Emily? Were you assaulted in any way?" Mont asked.

"Damn it, Mont," Lucas growled.

"I have to know, Lucas." Mont glanced at Emily. She shook her head. "You can shower then. After I finish here, I'll be over." Mont walked off.

Lucas put his arm around her shoulder and helped her to the truck. Emily felt light headed and stumbled. Lucas picked her up and carried her the rest of the way. He put her in the truck and drove her home. Once there, he carried her to the living room and put her on the couch. Munch jumped up beside her. Emily pulled her onto her lap and hugged her.

"I missed you, Munch." Emily gazed at Lucas. "Thank you for taking care of her." He nodded. "I do need a shower, Lucas. I've been in the basement for days. I'm so filthy."

Lucas nodded. "I'll help you."

She nodded. "All right." She stood and almost fell over. Lucas picked her up and carried her upstairs into the bathroom. He set her on her feet and undressed her. Lucas quickly undressed then turned on the shower. Munch pushed the door open and jumped up on the sink. She cleaned her paws as she gazed at Emily.

"I'm not letting you try to stand in here alone. I don't want you to fall so I'm going to hold you up. Then we're going to get some food in you." Lucas helped her into the shower.

The water felt like heaven to her. She placed her hands on the wall and hung her head under the water. Lucas stood behind her. Emily felt him pour shampoo in her hair and started working it into a lather. She felt the tears starting again and placed her hand over her mouth. Lucas turned her around to face him. Emily wrapped her arms around his waist and sobbed. He held her against him while she cried and murmured to her although she wasn't really listening. Her body shook as she cried.

"Emily, you're going to make yourself sick. Please baby, stop," he whispered.

"I can't st...stop." She stuttered as she laid her cheek on his chest.

He picked up the soap, lathered it up, and washed her. The hot water wasn't helping with her shaking. She knew she was in shock. After rinsing her off, he lifted her out and dried her off then he carried her to the bed and laid her on it. Munch jumped onto the bed and curled up next to Emily. Lucas was about to leave when she called his name. He turned to her.

"Please don't leave me, Lucas," she said softly.

He laid down beside her and kissed her forehead. "I won't," he whispered.

Emily was almost asleep when she heard someone pounding on the back door. She'd forgotten about Mont coming. Emily glanced toward Lucas and saw him awake too.

"It's probably the FBI," she told him.

"Yeah, it's Mont, for sure, and if I don't get down there and let him in, he'll kick the door in thinking something's wrong." Lucas sighed as he got off the bed. "Get dressed. Do you want me to help you down stairs? I'll make some coffee."

"I'm all right. Go let Mont in before he busts the door down."

* * * *

Lucas kissed her quickly and strode from the room and down the stairs. Opening the back door, he let his friend in. Mont raised an eyebrow at him.

"Is everything all right?" he asked.

"Yes. She fell asleep. She'll be down in a minute. You want some coffee?" When Mont nodded, Lucas went about making a pot.

Emily walked into the kitchen and sat at the table. She raised her eyes and stared at Mont. She frowned. "Montgomery?"

Mont's mouth twisted. "Mont. No one calls me Montgomery except my mother."

Emily smiled for the first time in days. "All right...Mont. Ask me any questions."

"Tell me about Walters taking you, what happened while you were in the house."

Emily took a deep breath and glanced at Mont. "I remember the explosion and someone putting a rag over my mouth and nose. The next thing I knew, I was in the basement of the house. Adam told me we were going to go away together after he took care of Lucas. But then he'd change his mind and say he was going to kill me." She glanced at her husband then back to Mont. "I told him I'd go away with him…" She stopped when Lucas hissed in a breath.

"Go on, Emily," Mont told her.

"I had no intention of going anywhere with him but I didn't want him to hurt Lucas. He didn't believe me anyway, and he said he'd kill me if I didn't go with him after he killed Lucas. Then he told me he changed his mind and was going to kill me after he killed Lucas." She shuddered. "He had my hands bound at first but later untied me so I could use the bathroom, but there was no way out of there other than the stairs. When Adam went outside to meet with Lucas, the two men told me they were planning to kill either Adam or Lucas, whoever survived. If you hadn't shown up when you did, I think they were planning to rape me." Her voice caught on a sob.

"*Son of a bitch!* If he doesn't die, I'll kill him," Lucas shouted.

"Calm down, Lucas. He'll get what he deserves," Mont said quietly as he stood. "So, basically you were just tied up in the basement until all this went down? You weren't assaulted at all?"

"He slapped me one time but that was all and it was when I refused to call Lucas."

Mont sighed. "All right. That's good enough for me. If you think of anything else, call me." He laid his card on the table and shook Lucas's hand. "Keep in touch, Lucas. It would be nice to hear from you other than when you need something."

"Fuck you, *Montgomery.*"

Mont burst out laughing, winked at Emily and left. She glanced up at Lucas. "Could you make me some soup? They didn't feed me much and all of a sudden I'm starving."

"That's good. I'll make it for you. Just sit there and look beautiful." Lucas smiled.

Emily ran her hand over her hair. "I doubt I can look beautiful after the past few days."

Lucas squatted down in front of her and took her hands in his. "You look beautiful to me. I haven't seen you in days. I've missed you so much." He leaned forward and kissed her.

"After I eat, I want to go to bed," she whispered.

Lucas nodded. "You need to rest."

She placed her hand on his whiskered cheek. "You don't understand. I want to go to bed…with you."

Lucas grinned. "I want you, too." He gave her a wink and stood. "Let me get the soup for you."

Emily smiled up at him. Dear God, she loved him so much and she'd almost lost him. It was time to let him know how she felt but after she ate. Not only was she hoping the soup would make her feel better, she hoped, in some way, it gave her the courage to tell her husband she was in love with him.

* * * *

Lucas made the soup for her, all the while keeping an eye on her. She seemed so weak. "What did they feed you?"

Emily snorted. "Crackers."

"That's it?" Lucas clenched his jaw.

"Adam said it was all they had." She shrugged. "I didn't have much of an appetite anyway."

Lucas knelt in front of her. "I'm so sorry I let him take you."

Emily gasped. "No. Lucas, it wasn't your fault. I told you he was smart. He probably watched us all the time and planned what to do." She gazed at him. "He told me he poisoned Star Gazer."

"Son of a bitch. I wish he was dead." Lucas rubbed the spot above his heart where the bullet had hit the vest. Without it, he would have died. He'd argued with Mont about wearing it but Mont told him he either wore it or didn't meet with Walters.

"I wish he was, too." Emily glanced at Lucas. "I want him out of my life. He'll go back to prison if he heals."

"Our lives," Lucas said. "He'll heal. They shot him in the leg and arm." He shook his head. "I should have watched better, though. I should have known when I heard the explosion, it was him, and he would get to you."

Emily placed her hands on his cheeks. "Please don't blame yourself. It's done and he's gone."

"If I would have given it some thought, I would have thought to take you with me, not leave you in the barn."

"Lucas, stop. I don't want to talk about it anymore. It was not your fault and that's the end of it."

Lucas blew out a breath. He knew he wasn't going to change her mind. Standing, he got her soup and set it on the table in front of her then sat down beside her. He watched as she ate.

"Stop staring at me, Lucas. I'm not going to disappear again," Emily snapped.

Lucas reared back. "I know. I'm just making sure you don't fall over. Christ, forgive me for being concerned."

"You're making me feel self-conscious about it."

"About it? What the fuck is *it*?"

Emily jumped up. "This." She waved her hands around. "All of it. I was taken but I'm home now. I want to forget it."

"I'm sure we both do but it won't go away in just a day or two." Lucas slowly stood and stared at her.

Her hands clenched into fists. "I am done talking about it." She started to move away from the table when Lucas wrapped his fingers around her bicep. She swung around and slapped him across the face.

Lucas quickly let go of her and stared at her. She stood in front of him with her hand over her mouth. Tears filled her eyes.

"Oh God! Lucas…I'm so sorry."

"It's all right. I shouldn't have grabbed you."

She shook her head. "You didn't *grab* me. You only put your hand on my arm. I...I panicked."

"I thought you said they didn't touch you?"

"They didn't. I'm just a little jumpy."

Lucas nodded. "Understandable." He ran his fingers through his hair. "Why don't you lie down? I'm going to the barn for a while. I'm sure Tinker will want to know you're all right."

"All right. Tell him I'll see him tomorrow." Emily left the room as Lucas headed toward the barn.

* * * *

Emily laid on the bed and more tears came. Munch jumped onto the bed and laid down beside her. Emily ran her hand over Munch's head.

"I missed you Munchkins. I missed Lucas too." The cat closed her eyes in bliss. "I'm so glad Adam will go back to prison." Munch started purring. Emily sat up. "You didn't growl when I said Adam." Emily shook her head. "Again, no growl." She laughed softly. "You know he's gone don't you? He'll never bother either of us again." She laid back down and closed her eyes. Nothing was better than being in her and Lucas's bed again. She'd missed him so much while she laid in the basement. Wondering if he were looking for her, missing her as she did him. She couldn't believe she'd slapped him. He looked as shocked as she'd felt. Emily fell asleep with Munch still purring beside her.

She woke up screaming. The bedroom door flew open and Lucas strode toward her. He sat on the bed beside her.

"Emily, are you all right?" he asked softly.

She nodded. "I just had a bad dream. I'm sorry I bothered you."

"You didn't bother me. I was getting some coffee."

"Coffee?" She frowned at him. "Why are you drinking coffee this late?" She glanced at the clock. It showed seven o'clock.

"It's seven in the morning, darlin'. You slept the rest of yesterday and last night."

"I did?" She was shocked.

"Yes. You needed it."

Emily glanced at the bed. "You didn't sleep with me?"

Lucas shook his head. "I didn't want to disturb you. I slept in another bedroom."

She threw her arms around his neck. "Please don't do that again. I want to always sleep with you."

His arms encircled her as he kissed her forehead. "All right." He stood.

"Where are you going?"

"I have work to do. Nick is out sick, we're shorthanded. I'll be in for lunch." He left the room leaving her staring after him.

She got up from the bed and took a shower then headed downstairs for coffee. She was feeling much better after sleeping so long. Munch wound through her legs as she walked to the table. Almost as soon as she sat down, there was a knock on the door.

Before she had a chance to open it, Tinker came marching in. He came right to her and sat down beside her. They gazed at each other with tears in their eyes. Tinker put his arms out and Emily leaned into them. She sobbed on his shoulder. Tinker patted her on the back, murmuring to her.

"It's all right, girl. You're home now. You're safe again. The son of a bitch is going back to prison and the world will be a better place."

Emily jerked back and laughed. "I have never heard you swear, Tinker."

Tinker's ears turned red. "I don't cuss around women but it's what he is."

Emily nodded. "Yes, he is. I'm glad it's over."

"You and me both. I know for sure Lucas is. He was a mad man while you were gone. Even that friend of his, the FBI agent, had trouble calming him down. I know I thought he was a bad penny when you first married him but he's turned into a great man. His friends too. They were here almost every day you were gone supporting him. They all grew into good men."

"Thank you, Tinker. I know Lucas respects you too. I'm happy you get along so well." She kissed his cheek. "I love you both and if you tell Lucas I said that, I'll deny it."

Tinker cackled. "I won't say anything but I think you should. That man loves you too."

Emily didn't correct him. She knew Lucas wasn't in love with her or he would have told her when she was rescued. Blinking back tears, she hugged Tinker again. "You'd better get back to work or your other boss will come looking for you."

Tinker laughed and stood. "I told him I was coming to see you whether he liked it or not. He just grinned." Tinker kissed her cheek. "Glad you're home safe and sound."

Emily watched him leave and smiled. She loved everyone at the ranch. They were her family and she hoped now that Adam was out of their lives, she and Lucas could start on their family in the near future. The blood drained from her face when she saw the sheriff's car pull up. Nathan stepped from the cruiser and strolled to the door.

Emily opened it before he got there. He took his hat off and smiled at her.

"How are you, Emily?" he asked.

"I'm fine. Come on in. Would you like some coffee?"

"Sure. Is Lucas in here?" Nathan took a seat at the table.

"No, but I can call him." Emily called the barn and asked Lucas to come to the house. She sat down beside Nathan and sipped her coffee. The back door opened and Lucas strolled in. He took his hat off and raised an eyebrow at her. She shrugged.

"What's up, Nathan?" Lucas asked as he poured himself a cup of coffee.

"We found two bodies down in a ditch off Center Road. One of them is Marylou."

Emily gasped. "I asked Adam if he knew where she was and he said no but I knew he was lying." She glanced at Nathan. "Who's the other woman?"

"A woman from Casper. Stella Carlisle. We found out she was visiting Adam while he was in prison. Surveillance shows her picking him up the day of his release."

"The bastard killed them," Lucas murmured.

Nathan nodded. "Yes. Ms. Carlisle had skin under her fingernails. It wasn't much but it was enough to show up as matching Walters' DNA." Nathan stood. "Marylou was shot in the head at close range while Miss Carlisle was strangled." He put his hat on. "Now, we can get him on murder charges. I wanted to tell you personally. You've been through a lot the past few days. I didn't want you to hear it through the Dry River grapevine." He nodded, shook their hands and left.

Emily glanced up at Lucas. "I think Nathan is one of the sexiest men I've ever seen. Him and his brother, Dakota are both hot. Mont is definitely sexy too."

"Maybe you should have asked one of them to marry you," Lucas smirked.

"Oh, Nathan's too busy to stay at the ranch and Dakota's in Colorado all the time. And you know Mont's in Jackson Hole." Emily grinned.

"Nathan's a good bit older than you too. He's in his late thirties and engaged."

Emily snorted. "Like it would make a difference." She laughed. "I'm just teasing. He is hot, though." She shook her head and sobered. "I think Adam became a little crazy in prison. He was verbally abusive but I'd have never thought he'd resort to murder."

Lucas crouched down in front of her. "He would have killed you, too."

Emily nodded. "Eventually. Whether he took me away with him or not. He would have gotten tired of me and just killed me." She shivered. "He's an evil man and he'll get what he deserves." She stood quickly. "I'm going to lie down."

Chapter Nine

Lucas watched her go and knew there was nothing he could do for her. She had to get past this on her own. He wanted to hold her and tell her it would all go away but it would be a lie. It was going to take her a while. Lucas took a seat at the table and sipped his coffee. Munch sat on the floor staring up at him. Lucas raised an eyebrow at her.

"What do you want, cat?"

Munch meowed up at him.

"I don't speak cat. Go away." Lucas pushed at her with his foot. Munch jumped onto his lap. Lucas almost spilled his coffee. "What the hell? Get down." He tried to push her off his lap but she laid down and curled into a ball. He glared down at her. "I don't like cats." He laid his hand on her to move her off his lap when he heard her purring. Lucas smiled. "I'm not so bad, either, am I?"

"I thought you didn't like cats?" Emily said from the doorway.

Lucas raised his eyebrow at her. "I thought you were going to lie down?"

Emily moved toward the cupboards and got tea and a cup down. "I got up there but didn't want to be alone. I feel better." She turned to face him. "You didn't answer my question." She nodded her head toward Munch.

"Just because she's on my lap, doesn't mean I like her."

Emily laughed softly. "Okay."

"She won't get down. Look at her," Lucas said.

"All you have to do is push her down. She'll give you a dirty look but she'll get over it." Emily leaned back against the countertop and grinned at Lucas.

"I don't need her growling at me. We need to live here together."

Emily laughed. "Uh huh."

Lucas glared at her. "Uh huh, what? You don't believe me?"

"No." Emily giggled.

Lucas pursed his lips. "My wife doesn't believe me, cat. What do you think? Do you think I like you?" Munch opened one eye and looked up at him then she closed it and fell back to sleep. Lucas glanced over to Emily. "Will you take her so I can go to work?"

Emily lifted Munch from Lucas's lap and cuddled the cat. Lucas kissed her quickly and headed for the barn.

* * * *

Two days later, Kendra came to visit along with their friend, Chloe Baxter. They sat in the living room, talking.

"I'm so sorry what happened to you, Emily," Chloe told her.

"I'm getting better, Chloe. I'm so glad he'll go back to prison. I hope he gets the death penalty for the murders."

"Me too. Thank God Wyoming has it. He's such a dick. I hate him."

Kendra and Emily were laughing when the back door opened and Lucas strolled into the living room. He stopped dead in his tracks when he saw the women. He removed his hat.

"I'm sorry. I didn't know you had company," he said.

"It's all right, Lucas. The girls just wanted to check up on me and visit for a while. Is there something you needed?"

"No. I thought if you were feeling better, we'd go for a ride, but we can go tomorrow." Emily smiled at him. Their eyes met and held until Kendra stifled a giggle. Lucas glanced away then back to her. "I'll just head back to the barn then." He spun on his heel and left.

The women looked at each other and laughed. Chloe sighed. "I had the biggest crush on Montgomery Bradford but I left to go to college and didn't get a chance to let him know I was interested." She stared at Emily. "What's he look like now?"

"Pffft. He's fat and bald now."

"*What?*" Chloe shouted.

Emily burst out laughing. "I'm kidding. He's gorgeous. Those green eyes of his." She sighed. "He's tall, probably around six four and built. Apparently being an FBI agent doesn't keep him chained to a desk."

"Wow. Now I wish you hadn't told me the truth." Chloe pouted.

"Lucas is gorgeous, Emily. It must be such a hardship being married to him." Kendra teased.

Emily turned toward her. "Speaking of gorgeous, what the hell is going on between you and Cooper? You two didn't even acknowledge each other when Lucas and I got married."

Kendra's cheeks reddened. "We don't like each other much." She shrugged.

Chloe burst out laughing. "Oh, please. Tell her the truth, Kennie. You have the hots for Cooper."

"You do?" Emily asked as she looked at Kendra. "Still?"

Kendra shrugged. "He broke my heart, though. I can't get past the fact he hurt my feelings. He was so cruel about it. I was fifteen and had a huge crush on him. I saw him with Debbie Lawson and I was so jealous, I asked him the next day what he saw in her and he smiled and said 'what do you think?' I told him I was sure there were other girls much nicer. He laughed and told me if I was thinking of myself to get over it. I was still a baby." She shook her head. "It really hurt me. I just never got over him being so cruel."

"You never told me about it. Why not?" Emily asked.

Kendra shrugged. "You were so wrapped up in the ranch. Cooper came to see me the next day. He said he wanted to apologize and he meant nothing by it, I was just too young for him."

"He was sorry, Kennie. You should have given him the chance to prove it." Chloe raised an eyebrow.

"I was young and hurt, Chloe. How do I even know he's changed?"

Chloe snorted. "I still think you should have listened to him."

"I told him we'd forget what happened and move on with our lives. What more do you want?"

"How about giving the guy a chance to make it up to you? He's gorgeous."

"Girls, girls. Please stop." Emily interrupted. "If Kendra wants to get past her time with Cooper, it's none of our business, Chloe."

"Fine. Maybe I'll go after him myself then." At Kendra's gasp, Chloe smirked and pointed at Kendra. "See? She still wants him."

Emily laughed. "Stop, Chloe."

Chloe stood. "She knows I love her. Let's get going so Emily can rest." She turned to Emily. "You look tired."

"I am. I'll walk out with you and then I'll lie down." The women walked out the front door and Emily watched as her friends left. Too bad Lucas couldn't lie down too.

* * * *

Lucas worked in the barn for a few more hours before he finished up for the day. Tinker stood at one of the stalls. Lucas stopped beside him.

"I'm heading in. I need to catch up on some sleep. I'm exhausted," Lucas told him.

"I'm sure you are. Is Emily getting some rest?"

Lucas sighed. "She's trying, but she keeps having nightmares. She wakes up in a cold sweat every night." Lucas shook his head. "She's fine during the day, but once night falls, she freaks."

"It was hard on her." Tinker nodded.

"I think a lot of it has to do with her being held in that basement. Mont said it was dark and damp down there." He slapped Tinker on the shoulder. "She'll get back to her old self soon enough."

"I hope so. I miss her out here." Tinker walked down the barn aisle while Lucas moved toward the house.

He entered the back door and noticed how quiet the house was. He figured she was taking a nap and he was ready to join her after a shower. He slowly climbed the stairs and entered the bathroom to undress. He came to a halt when he saw her in the tub with her head back and eyes closed. Lucas squatted down beside the tub and touched her cheek. Her eyes snapped open then she smiled at him.

"Hi. I didn't hear you come in."

"How long have you been in there?" Lucas asked.

"I'm not sure. What time is it?"

"A little after five."

"I just got in here a few minutes ago. I dozed off." She smiled. "I'm so tired."

"You haven't been sleeping much."

"I know and because of it you haven't either. I'm sorry," Emily whispered as she touched his cheek. "You need a shave, Mister Taggart."

"I need you, Missus Taggart." He leaned forward and pressed his lips to hers. When she moaned against his lips, he deepened the kiss. His tongue moved against the seam of her lips. He growled when she opened to him.

Emily pulled back from him. "Get me out of here."

Lucas grinned and stood. He reached into the tub, put his hands under her arms, and lifted her out. After setting her on the rug beside the tub, he reached for a fluffy white towel and dried her off before carrying her to the bedroom. He laid her on the bed and quickly shed his clothes but hesitated.

"I need a shower. I just came in from the barn," he told her.

"I like you sweaty, get in the bed." She raised her arms to him.

Lucas groaned and got on the bed with her and pulled her into his arms. "I've missed you so much." He pressed his lips to hers and took them in a deep kiss.

Emily groaned into his mouth. When she moved her tongue into his mouth, he moaned deep in his throat.

"I'll never get enough of you, Emily. Never."

"Lucas, I..." His mouth stopped her from saying more. He pulled back from her and gazed down into her face.

"You are the most beautiful woman I've ever known. There's no other to compare to you. I'll cherish you for the rest of my life. I love you Emily," he whispered.

"What?" Her eyes widened as she gazed up at him.

"I love you. I know you don't love me yet but maybe one day--"

Emily laughed. "I do love you, Lucas. So much."

"Wait. What? You do?"

She nodded her head. "I have for a while now."

Lucas glared at her. "And you didn't tell me?"

Emily raised her eyebrows. "You didn't tell me. I wasn't about to put my feelings out there and make you uncomfortable."

Lucas laughed. "I wouldn't have felt uncomfortable. I would've felt wonderful because I loved you too." He chuckled. "Damn, my wife is hardheaded."

Emily giggled. "Yes but she has nothing on her husband as far as stubbornness goes."

He sobered. "I was so scared when you were gone. I wanted to kill him and if Mont hadn't been with me, I would've found you and killed him." He swallowed hard. "I don't know what I would've done if he'd taken you away from me, in any way. Mont knew I was in love with you and I was going crazy without you."

Lucas watched as tears rolled down her face. "I was scared, too. When he called you to make you go there, I was terrified. I know he wanted to kill you. I'm so glad Mont made you wear the vest but when I saw you lying on the ground, I wanted to die if you were dead. Lucas, I need you in my life and like you said, I can't remember what my life was like before you came into it."

Lucas moved to kiss her when Munch butted her head against him. Lucas narrowed his eyes and glared at her. "Go away, cat."

"You really should start calling her Munch since you like her," Emily snorted.

"Who said I like her?"

Emily grinned. "Love me, love my cat."

Lucas laughed softly. "Now you're pushing it." He pressed his lips to hers and made both of them forget the terror they'd gone through.

* * * *

Adam laid in the hospital bed, thinking. There was no way he was going back to prison. He was going to get away and this time he would kill them both. The wound in his leg wasn't so bad but the one in his arm hurt like a bitch, but not enough to keep him from getting them back. If they thought two small gunshot wounds would keep him from his agenda, they had another think coming. He would get out of here one way or another and kill them this time.

He sat up when a pretty nurse entered his room. He smiled at her. She blushed as she checked his IV.

"Do you need any pain killers?" she asked him.

"I'm fine, thank you." He grinned up at her.

The young nurse smiled and left. Adam watched as she stopped at the doorway to talk to the FBI agent stationed at his door. She grinned up at him and flirted. The agent seemed to flirt back. This could work in Adam's favor. He watched as the agent kept his eyes on her backside as she walked away.

"She sure is a looker," Adam said.

The agent turned to glare at him. "Shut up."

Adam laughed. "Hell, I'd go for it if I was out of this bed. You should take her up on what she's offering."

"Do I need to close this door so I don't have to listen to your mouth?"

Adam shook his head. "No." He shrugged. "I just thought she looked like she was really interested in you."

"Mind your own fucking business," The agent told him.

Shit! Obviously, it wouldn't work with this agent, but another was due to come on duty in a few minutes and Adam knew he was very young and inexperienced. He'd taken the shift yesterday after the agent at the door now. Adam was sure he could get him to walk away from the door for a while. A few minutes later, he grinned as he saw the young agent talking with the other one. The older agent gave Adam a glare before he left for the day.

Adam waited two hours before he called for a nurse. A small, petite blonde-haired woman entered the room.

"What do you need?"

"I could use a pain killer," Adam told her as he glanced toward the door. "I think that agent likes you." He chuckled.

The nurse looked toward the door then back to him. "What makes you say that?"

"He can't keep his eyes off you. How long have you been a nurse?"

"I just graduated." Her gaze traveled back to the agent.

Adam was elated. She and the agent were both young and inexperienced. "Maybe you should talk to him."

She blushed. "Oh, I can't do that, I'm on duty and so is he." She handed Adam a pill, then his water.

Adam nodded. "Sure. Well, maybe when you take a break." He tossed the pill in his mouth and took a sip of water but didn't swallow the pill.

She nodded and left the room, smiling at the agent as she did. He smiled back. Adam chuckled. He was sure he'd be out of here tonight.

* * * *

Later in the afternoon, Emily exercised Cinnamon in the inside corral while Lucas shoed one of the other horses. Every once in a while, he'd glance over to her to make sure she was doing all right. She was getting stronger as the days passed. Knowing Lucas loved her helped tremendously. As she rode Cinnamon around the corral, she glanced toward the barn to see Nathan follow Tinker into the barn. Emily dismounted and moved toward Lucas. He grinned at her. She nodded toward Nathan and saw Lucas frown when he saw him too. Lucas took her hand as they waited for Nathan to get to them.

Nathan halted in front of them and sighed. "Walters escaped from the hospital."

Emily gasped. "When?"

"About an hour ago. There's an APB out on him."

"How the hell did he walk out of the hospital? There was an agent posted at his room," Lucas spoke through clenched teeth.

"Apparently the agent took a break with a nurse and was gone for quite a while." Nathan shook his head. "I'd hate to be him when Mont gets a hold of him."

"*Son of a bitch!*" Lucas pulled Emily behind him. "We need to get into the house."

Nathan nodded. "Yes and don't come out until we contact you. Mont will probably be out here tomorrow. He'll protect you but for tonight, I can send a deputy out."

"Please do, Nathan," Emily whispered.

"I'll call it in and I'll stay until he gets here. Let's go inside."

Emily thought she was going to pass out. Lucas squeezed her hand as he led her to the house. Once inside, she moved to the living room and sat in the window seat.

"Emily, please move away from the window." Nathan requested.

"Why?" she asked.

Nathan glanced at Lucas then back to her. "I don't want to alarm you but Walters could be out there watching you."

Emily quickly moved from the window and sat in one of the wingback chairs. Lucas strode to the window and pulled the drapes closed. He then moved to each window and closed the blinds and drapes. Emily watched his every movement. The thought of Adam being out there again more than terrified her. She started shaking and couldn't stop. Lucas sat on the arm of the chair and rubbed her back.

"He won't get near us, Emily. I won't let him take you from me again." He kissed the top of her head.

Emily nodded but she knew Adam would be determined to get to her and Lucas both. He would be hell bent on killing them both this time. Nothing and no one would stop him. She gazed up at Lucas.

"He'll kill us both."

Lucas shook his head. "No. I won't let that happen."

Nathan moved toward the door when a cruiser pulled up. He glanced at Emily and Lucas. "I'll be right back."

Lucas moved toward the door but stayed behind it as he watched Nathan speak with his deputy. They both moved toward the house. Nathan entered with the deputy behind him.

"Lucas, this is Deputy Marshall Hicks."

Lucas stared at the deputy then glanced at Nathan. "Has he been on the force long?"

"He's been in law enforcement for fifteen years. He'll protect you until Mont gets here tomorrow," Nathan told him.

Lucas nodded and shook the deputy's hand. "Have you talked to Mont?" He asked Nathan.

"Yes. To say he's pissed would be an understatement. I can't imagine what he said to the agent who fucked up." Nathan shook hands with Lucas. "Don't go outside unless it can't be avoided. I prefer neither of you leave this house at all. I'm going to talk to Tinker and the guys to alert them. I don't trust the son of a bitch. He'll do what he can to get to you both and he won't let anyone stand in his way. I wish I had more men to spare but I don't." He gave them an abrupt nod and left.

* * * *

Lucas pulled Emily out of the chair then sat down and set her on his lap. She laid her head on his shoulder. He rubbed her arms and murmured to her trying to comfort her. He was sure he wasn't doing much good with the way she was still shaking. Lucas didn't know what to do to comfort her. With Walters out there, Lucas and Emily couldn't take a chance and leave the house. With only one deputy to guard them until Mont arrived, Lucas was going to have to be on guard also. Lucas knew Nathan had informed Tinker and the men to stay alert and report anything out of the ordinary but Lucas knew what Walters was capable of even if he was alone. Lucas knew he was out there now, watching and waiting.

"You should go lie down, darlin'," Lucas whispered.

"I don't want to be alone."

Deputy Hicks glanced out the window then back to Lucas. "Both of you should get some rest. It's going to be a long night."

Lucas nodded. "Come on Emily, let's go upstairs and take a nap." He stood with her in his arms and carried her. At the door to their bedroom, he lightly kissed her lips then carried her to the bed and laid down beside her.

"It'll be all right."

Emily nodded and put her arms around his neck. "I hope so Lucas. I really hope so."

Lucas pulled her tightly against him. When it thundered outside, Emily jumped.

"It's just thunder, baby. It's going to storm. That should keep him away through the night."

"He won't let it stop him," Emily whispered.

Lucas didn't say any more, he held her. It was all he knew to do for now. If Walters came near them then he'd protect her with his life if it came down to it. He'd die before he let Walters take her from him again.

* * * *

Adam Walters watched the house through binoculars. One deputy wasn't going to stop him from getting to them, but the men at the ranch were sure to be on the lookout. With the storm moving in it may be a lot easier than he'd planned on. The rumbling thunder would cover the sounds of a gun. He smiled as the thunder moved in closer. Lightening flashed, lighting up the darkening sky. Tonight, as the storm raged, he'd make his move. He got up, ran into the woods alongside the house, and took shelter in a cave. No one would find him there. As he moved into the cave, he used a lighter he'd stolen at the hospital to see with. Also, some blankets and scrubs to put on under his clothes for the night. It still got chilly at night. He'd get a fire built and take a quick nap. It would be over tonight.

* * * *

Emily tried to sleep but she was too afraid to close her eyes. Adam would make a move tonight, she was sure of it. The storm would help him more than hinder him. He'd use it to his advantage. She knew that without a doubt. He was crafty, evil, and smart.

"Please relax darlin'. We're probably going to be up all night. I'll have to help the deputy guard the house. He can't do it alone."

"I won't sleep without you beside me, Lucas."

Lucas laughed softly. "I know. It's why you need to nap now. I know you'll be downstairs with me."

She nodded. "You know me too well, Mister Taggart."

"Damn straight I do, Missus Taggart." Lucas kissed her forehead. "I love you."

"I love you too, Lucas. So much."

He kissed her softly. "We'll be fine. I won't let him get to you. I'll die first."

Emily gasped. "No. I won't let that happen. I just found you, I won't lose you."

"Then we'll have to take him down first."

"Yes, we will." She moved off the bed and proceeded into the walk-in closet. She came back out carrying a locked box. "I have a pistol in here that granddaddy bought for me years ago. I never liked guns but he made me learn how to shoot." She opened the box and held up the pistol to show Lucas.

He strolled over to her, took the pistol from her, and whistled. "Nice. A Glock G17. That's some gun. It's well over five hundred dollars." He grinned. "Remind me never to piss you off."

Emily laughed. "I'd never shoot you, Lucas. If I get mad at you, I'd just withhold sex."

"Aww, hell. I'd rather be shot," Lucas muttered.

Emily burst out laughing. "You would think that way."

Lucas jerked her against him and took her lips in a deep kiss. "I have a weapon too but it's in the office in the barn. I need to get it."

"No. You aren't going outside, Lucas." Emily put her hands on her hips and glared at him.

"I need my gun, Emily."

"I'll get you one from the gun cabinet in the office."

Lucas narrowed his eyes at her then nodded. "I want to pick it out, though." He grabbed her hand. "Let's go."

Emily followed him down the stairs to the office. Once inside, she moved to the desk and removed a key from another locked box. She then unlocked the gun cabinet and waved for Lucas to pick out a pistol.

He stepped forward and gazed at the guns. Finally, he reached for one and showed it to her, smiling. "I like your Glock G17, so I'm taking the same thing." He sobered. "I'd like to unload all seventeen into him."

They both jumped when they heard the deputy behind them. "You two aren't planning to go all Rambo on me, are you?" He leaned against the doorjamb and folded his arms.

"Are you married, deputy?" Lucas asked him.

"Yes, I am. Been married almost ten years. Why?"

"If someone was trying to hurt your wife, what would you do?"

Deputy Hicks smiled. "Touché." He pushed away from the door. "I understand but let's not get all gung-ho about it. We'll see how it goes. I'm hoping he won't show up until after the FBI gets here and we have more men."

They all jumped when thunder boomed over the house. Emily let out a little scream and wrapped her arms around Lucas.

"It's just thunder," Lucas said, and then frowned. "That could be on his side. Couldn't it?" He looked at the deputy.

"Yes. I thought that earlier when the storm started." He shrugged. "We'll have to be on our toes. Bad thing is, your men are stuck in the barn and have no way of seeing anything with the way the rain's coming down."

Lucas moved to the phone on the desk and dialed the barn. "Nick? Is everything all right out there?" Lucas nodded. "All right. I'll check in again later." He turned to the deputy. "Nick said they were all playing cards but making checks every fifteen minutes.

They're going out and checking around but haven't seen anything."
He moved to sit down when the lights went out.

* * * *

The power went out making Emily scream. Lucas opened the
desk drawer and took out a flashlight. He shined it around the room.
"Stay calm. It could be the storm." He moved around the desk. "Sit
down here and don't move." He headed toward the door but stopped
when he heard Emily behind him. "Go sit down."

"I'm not staying here alone."

"Close the door behind me and lock it. I know I can leave you
here alone. Walters won't get past me to get to this room if he tries
to come in. If the power's off because of him." Lucas was almost to
the door when the power came back on. He let out a relieved breath.
He spun around to see Emily still behind him. He raised an eyebrow
at her.

"I was going to lock the door," she told him.

"Now why don't I believe you?" He grinned.

Emily blushed as she gazed up at her husband. "You don't
believe me?"

"Not for a second." Lucas kissed her quickly. "You will not do
anything like that again. Am I clear? I can't have you thinking you
can follow me. Just what do you plan on doing?"

"I have a gun, Lucas. I want to help."

Lucas put the gun in the back of his waistband and put his hands
on her shoulders. "I only want you to use the gun if you absolutely
have to. I don't want you running out of the house for any reason.
Not to follow the deputy or me. You will stay put if something
happens." He lightly shook her. "You get it?"

"Yes." Emily smiled sadly. "But I won't hesitate to shoot him if
he comes in this house or hurts you."

Lucas burst out laughing and pulled her against him. "That's my
girl."

Deputy Hicks entered the room. "I didn't see anything to
suggest it was Walters. Call the barn, Mister Taggart, and check on
them."

Lucas nodded and dialed the barn. "Joe, is everything all right
out there?" Lucas listened then nodded to Hicks. "All right, I'll keep

checking with you." He hung up. "He said the lights went out and the men ran out to the yard but when they saw the house lights were out, they were sure it was from the storm. The two breakers are on different circuits."

"Why didn't they call the house though to check?" Emily asked.

"Joe said they were just getting ready to," Lucas told her.

Emily sighed and left the office, heading toward the living room. Lucas followed her.

"I'm going to lie down on the sofa for a while. I'm so tired but I don't want to go upstairs. I feel safer down here."

Lucas nodded and took a seat in the wingback chair. He picked up the TV remote and flipped it on. Stretching out his long legs in front of him, he clasped his hands across his flat stomach and tried to watch what was on but it held no appeal. He wanted to be out there looking for Walters. Lucas turned his head to look for Hicks and saw him checking out the windows. The man seemed to be constantly in motion. Always alert. It made Lucas feel a little better. He glanced over to see Emily sleeping. Good. She needed to sleep. It was hard to tell what the night would bring.

He stood and headed for the kitchen to make a sandwich. Not that he was hungry but he needed his strength. Walters would not have any kind of advantage over him. Hicks strolled into the kitchen and glanced out the backdoor. "Damn, the rain is getting harder."

"Do you want a sandwich, deputy?" Lucas asked as he got lunchmeat out of the refrigerator.

"I could eat," Hicks said as he kept an eye out.

Lucas made them both sandwiches and they sat at the table to eat. Neither man said much, lost in his own thoughts. When thunder shook the house, Lucas jumped. Hicks didn't move.

"You're not nervous at all, are you?" Lucas said.

Hicks shook his head. "Been a cop too long. I used to work in Detroit as a detective." He shrugged. "I've just about seen it all."

"Yeah, I suppose you have then. That's a big city."

Hicks nodded. "That it is. Nothing like here. Dry River could fit in the center of Detroit and still have room."

"You've been in law enforcement for fifteen years?"

"Yes. I had to get out of the big city. I happened to be driving to Oregon and saw the sign for Dry River. I wasn't in any hurry, so I thought I'd see the little town. I stopped at Jonesy's and a fight broke out. Nathan arrived but couldn't handle all three men, so I helped him. We got talking and he offered me a job. I took it. He's never asked why I left the force in Detroit." Hicks shook his head. "Not once."

"Nathan trusts you and he probably doesn't feel like it's his business. He's a good guy. His brother, Dakota, and I are best friends. We ran around together when we were younger. Raised a lot of hell. Nathan always tried to get us to settle down but we never listened. He's only six years older than us but he was so much more mature."

Hicks nodded. "He certainly has his head on straight. Helluva guy."

"Have you met his fiancée?"

"Shelly is the woman for him, that's for sure."

The men talked well into the night, with Hicks making his rounds every half hour. He walked around the porch. When he came back in, he told Lucas the rain was making it too dark to see, even with lights on in the yard.

Lucas glanced out the back door and gazed up at the yard lights. The rain came down in sheets. As he stood there looking at the lights, one went out. Lucas straightened up. The second light went out then the third. The yard was pitch black.

"The yard lights went out. One at a time," Lucas said softly.

Hicks moved to the door. "Move away from the door and call the barn."

Lucas nodded as he moved toward the phone. The glass in the backdoor shattered. Hicks hit the floor. Lucas got down on the floor.

"Hicks, are you hit?" Lucas whispered.

"No. Can you call the barn?" Hicks crawled toward him. "Tell them not to come out for any reason, unless we call them again. Walters could pick them off."

Lucas called the barn. "Joe, keep all the guys in the barn. Walters is here. He's shooting into the house. I don't want anyone to come out of there, you got it?" Lucas listened. "Good. I'll call you back when I can."

Lucas crawled to the living room just as the lights went out again. This time he knew it was Walters. Thunder clapped overhead and a shot whizzed above his head. He hit the floor.

"Emily," he shouted.

"Don't yell for her. We don't want her to stand up and take a chance at getting shot."

Shit! Lucas hadn't even thought of that. He got up to all fours again and made his way quickly toward Emily. He reached her and gently touched her shoulder. She moaned.

"Emily, come on darlin'. Wake up." Lucas shook her shoulder.

"Lucas? What is it?"

He pulled her to the floor. She let out a surprised shriek. "Lucas. What are you doing? Why are the lights...? Oh God. He's here, isn't he?"

"Yes. He shot out the yard lights and then killed the house lights." Gunfire shattered the front window. Lucas felt Emily shaking as he wrapped his arms around her. "Stay down."

"Where's the deputy?" Emily whispered.

"Hicks," Lucas shouted.

"I'm still in the kitchen. I'm going out to the porch. Stay put."

Lucas practically laid on top of Emily to protect her. She put her hands over her ears as more shots rang out. Lucas heard glass breaking as the shots hit items in the house. "*Son of a bitch!* Come with me." He pulled Emily behind him to the hallway and put her back against the wall. "We're safe here."

Emily wrapped her arms around him. "Please don't leave me."

"I won't." More shots rang out and Lucas heard a loud grunt as someone hit the porch floor. "Shit. I hope that wasn't Hicks." He pulled away from Emily. "I'll be right back."

"You just said you wouldn't leave me. Lucas, no."

"Where's your gun?"

"On the coffee table."

"I'll be right back with it. Do not move." Lucas crawled away from her and returned a few minutes later. "Here. Take the safety off and keep it in front of you. I have to check on Hicks, he might need help. I won't be long but I can't leave him out there."

"You're right. Just please be careful." When he started to move away from her, she grabbed his arm. "Please come back to me, Lucas."

"I will." He kissed her hard and fast then crawled away. Lucas slowly moved out of the hallway toward the foyer. The leaded glass in the front door provided no light to the porch. The rain pounded on the tin roof of the house, making it almost impossible to hear. A shot shattered the glass in the door. Lucas moved back quickly as the sidelights splintered into shards. Next, the windows across the front of the house shattered.

"Damn it," Lucas muttered as he crawled to the living room to try to get out of the line of fire. Then he crawled back to the hall entrance. "I'm going to slide my phone to you, along the wall."

"All right," Emily whispered. "Are you okay?"

"Yes but the bastard's shooting all the windows out. Stay alert. Call Nathan then the barn and tell Joe and Nick to come out but be careful. Walters is still at the front of the house." He hesitated. "Emily, please keep the gun in front of you. You know how to shoot. I love you."

"I love you too, Lucas. Please be careful."

Lucas crawled back toward the front door, reached up, and put his hand on the knob. Turning it slowly, he pulled the door open and glanced out. He couldn't see anything but he did hear moaning. It was Hicks. *Fuck!* Lucas had to get out there and help him. He lowered himself to his stomach and crawled out toward the direction he heard the moaning. More gunfire rang out. Lucas put his arms over his head and waited for it to stop. The bastard had to reload sometime. As soon as it stopped, Lucas crawled toward Hicks and finally reached him.

"Hicks, how bad is it?" Lucas whispered.

"Just my shoulder but I'm losing a lot of blood."

Lucas nodded then realized Hicks couldn't see him. "I told Emily to call Nathan."

"Good. He'll know to come in silent."

I'm going to drag you inside the house," Lucas told him.

"No. You go back in. If he steps on this porch, I'll get him."

The gunfire stopped. Lucas glanced around. "He's shot all the front windows out."

"I have a feeling he's not done." As soon as Hicks spoke, gunfire started again, this time around the side of the house. "He's going to circle the house and shoot them all out."

"Why?"

"He's going to come in through one of them." Hicks groaned. "Get inside with your wife. I imagine she's scared to death. Go. I'll be fine. Nathan will be here soon."

Lucas didn't like leaving him on the porch but he had no choice, he had to get back to Emily. He could hear the back windows shattering as the bullets went through them, so he stood and ran for the hallway. Stopping at the entrance to the hall, he softly called out her name.

"Emily? It's me. I'm coming back to you."

"Please hurry." Her voice caught on a sob.

Lucas ran to her and sat down beside her. He pulled her into his arms.

"Is deputy Hicks all right?"

"He's been shot in the shoulder. He needs to get to a hospital before he loses too much more blood."

"Can we get him in here?" Emily was shaking.

"I wanted to drag him in but he said to leave him. I don't know where Walters is right now." Lucas looked toward the end of the hallway. "He's shooting all the windows out so he can come in one of them. I think if we stay here, we'll see him no matter which direction he comes from."

Emily screamed when the gunfire started again, this time in the kitchen area. She put her hands over her ears and moved closer to Lucas. As the windows on the side of the house shattered, Lucas heard more shots coming from a different direction. He started to move away from Emily when she grabbed him.

"Where are you going?"

"Nathan must be here. The other shots are coming from the front of the house. I want to get Hicks in here and out of danger." He kissed her forehead. "I'll be right back. Stay here."

"No. What if Adam gets in?"

"Shoot the bastard." Lucas crawled away from her.

* * * *

Emily held the pistol in both hands and kept glancing in both directions of the hallway. She was terrified Adam was going to enter the house and find her. Her hands were shaking so badly, she held onto the gun with both hands. She heard more gunshots coming from the front of the house then silence.

"Lucas," she shouted. He didn't answer. She started to get to her knees when she heard glass crunching under shoes from the direction of the office. It had to be Adam. Lucas had gone out the front and she knew he'd let her know if he was coming back in. She started scooching back toward the living room end of the hallway when the footsteps halted. A beam of light hit her in the eyes. Emily threw her hand up to shade her face.

"Well, look what we have here," Adam laughed.

Emily gasped. "Get away from me. Lucas will be here in a minute."

"Oh I don't think so. I already took care of him. Get up. You're going with me."

"I'm not going anywhere with you," She shouted as she quickly stuck her gun in the back of her waistband.

Adam reached down, grabbed her hair, and pulled her to her feet. "Yes you are. I have to get out of here before they figure out I'm in the house and you're going with me."

"Do you seriously think they're going to let you just walk out of here?"

He sneered at her. "I have you, remember?" He pulled her behind him. "Now, come on."

"Did you kill Lucas?" Emily asked in a choked voice.

"He's dead. Come on."

Emily screamed and kicked him. Adam let go of her. She backed away from him and reached for the gun. When she pulled it out and pointed it at him, he came to a dead stop and grinned.

"You don't have the balls," he said as he stepped toward her.

Emily aimed and fired at him. He had a look of surprise on his face when the bullet struck him. Adam looked down at the bloodstain on his shirt and back to her. He made another move toward her. She shot again. This time he fell to the ground and didn't move. She stood staring at him lying on the floor when someone reached around her and took the gun out of her hands.

"It's over, darlin'. Come on."

Emily glanced over her shoulder to see Lucas standing behind her. "Lucas..." was all she said before she fainted.

Chapter Ten

Lucas caught her before she fell and carried her to the couch. He gently laid her down. Nathan came striding into the room with smelling salts and after breaking it open, he waved it under Emily's nose. She pushed at his hand, opened her eyes, and blinked up at Lucas.

"Lucas?" she whispered.

"Yes?" He sat on the coffee table. "What is it?"

Emily sat up and touched his face. "You're all right?" He nodded and she threw her arms around his neck and sobbed.

Lucas wrapped his arms around her and glanced up at Nathan, who shrugged. "I'm fine. What is it?"

Emily pulled back from him. "He said you were dead."

"Son of a bitch," Lucas muttered. "I imagine he lied to get you to go with him."

"I told him I wasn't going anywhere with him. I hid my gun before he saw it and when he pulled me up, I kicked him and pulled my gun out." She gazed at Lucas with tear-filled eyes. "I shot him. He said I didn't have the balls but I shot him. Twice."

Nathan sat down beside her on the couch. "I'll need to get a statement from you. Can you come to the station tomorrow?" At her nod, he stood. "I'll get the coroner out here then we'll let you get some rest."

Emily glanced at him. "How's Deputy Hicks?"

Nathan smiled. "He'll be fine, thanks to Lucas here. He kept pressure on the wound." Nathan nodded and moved outside to call for the coroner.

"I let him get to you again. I didn't do a very good job at protecting you, did I?" Lucas whispered.

"Don't say that. You kept me sane all these months and now it's over."

"He got to you again. I had no idea he was in the house. He made it look like he'd taken off for the woods."

"How did he do that?" Emily frowned at him.

"He ran off in that direction. Nathan ran after him, leaving one deputy out front with Joe and Nick at the back. Walters circled back to the side of the house. Fooled us all." Lucas shook his head.

Emily put her hand on his. "It doesn't matter now. He's dead and out of our lives for good."

Lucas nodded. "Yes."

"Lucas Taggart, you stop this right now. If you hadn't helped Deputy Hicks, he may have died or if you'd have stayed with me, we could both be dead. Adam wasn't going to let either of us live. He came into this house with the intention of killing us. He didn't know you weren't in the house until he heard me call for you."

Lucas pulled her into his arms and kissed her. "I don't know what I would've done if he'd have hurt you."

"I thought I was going to die when he said you were dead." She shuddered against him. "I didn't want to live if you were gone."

Lucas kissed the tears from her eyes. "I'm here. I'll always be here."

* * * *

The next day, Lucas let Mont in the back door. Mont glanced around then stared at Lucas. "I'm glad you two are all right. He shot out the windows, huh?"

"Yes. Nathan seems to think he was doing it to throw us off on how he'd come in."

Mont nodded. "That's exactly what he was doing." He huffed. "I'm sorry you had to go through that, Lucas. The son of a bitch should've never walked out of the hospital."

"So, does the agent have any ass left after you chewed him a new one?"

"Not enough to sit on. He's in a lot of trouble and so is the nurse. If he'd have thought with his head instead of his dick, Walters would be in prison now."

"He's better off dead," Lucas muttered.

"You won't get an argument from me, but it's no excuse he was able to walk right out of there. He was hell bent on killing you both and he didn't care who he took down to get to you. Deputy Hicks will be out for a while leaving Nathan shorthanded."

Lucas sighed. "I know. Deputy Hicks is a good man. I'm sorry he was shot."

Mont grunted. "Perks of the job. I'm just glad no one but Walters was killed."

Lucas made coffee and Mont sat down at the table and glanced around. "Has Nathan taken pictures? I have Tucker outside getting some now. He'll need to get some in here too."

Emily entered the kitchen, Mont and Lucas stood. She waved them down. "Hello Mont."

"Emily, I'm sorry--" Mont began.

"It's not your fault, Montgomery," Emily said.

Mont winced. "Now I know I'm in trouble."

Emily laughed. "No, you're not in trouble. I'm being honest when I say it wasn't your fault. The 'Montgomery' just slipped out."

Mont grinned. "All right but I should have put a more experienced man there. Agent Straus is a veteran with the FBI, but Agent Williams isn't. Agent Straus told me Walters tried a mind game on him too." Mont shrugged. "He didn't fall for it, but Agent Williams apparently did."

"It's over and done with Mont. Walters is dead and we can on move past this," Lucas said.

Mont gave a nod. "I'll send Agent Tucker in when he's done outside. I just want this for my file since we didn't get here in time to help last night. I'll talk with you soon, Lucas." He glanced at Emily. "I'm glad you're all right." He left the house.

Lucas strolled over to Emily and wrapped his arms around her. "I'm glad it's over with. We can move on now."

"Yes." She gazed up at him. "I want to have a baby, Lucas."

Lucas grinned. "I'd love to start on a family right now but we have to wait until everyone clears out of here." He chuckled when she blushed.

"You love making me blush, don't you?"

"That I do, darlin'. That I do."

* * * *

Emily watched as Lucas left the kitchen and headed for the barn. She saw him stop and talk with Tinker. She smiled as she realized how much she loved both men. Turning from the door, she headed for the back office but came to a halt when she saw the blood in the hallway. Agent Tucker was snapping pictures and writing things in a tablet. He glanced up at her.

"I don't want you to come back here yet, Missus Taggart. The sheriff wants to get pictures too, and we can't disturb this area."

Emily nodded. "I understand." She felt sick to her stomach looking at the blood. Was she going to have to clean it up? Oh, Lord she hoped not. She'd be sick for sure. Maybe she could talk Lucas into doing it. Smiling, she moved toward the living room and sat in the window seat. It would be June in another week. The grass was green and the hydrangea bushes running along the front of the porch were beginning to bud. The large oak trees provided the front porch with shade. Emily couldn't wait to sit on the front porch in one of the wooden rocking chairs there. Maybe one day, holding her child against her as she rocked or watching Lucas rock their baby. She noticed a big truck coming up the driveway followed by several pickup trucks. She walked out onto the porch and watched as they pulled around the side of the house.

Emily ran through the house to the back and out the door. Lucas came striding from the barn, smiling. The biggest truck had lumber and new windows on it. The pickup trucks carried Lucas's friends. They all hopped out and waved at her. She waved back but turned to face Lucas as he stood at the bottom of the porch steps.

"What's going on?"

"I ordered new windows so we can replace the ones shot out. The guys are here to help install them." He shrugged. "They're cheap labor."

"We will work for food, however," Dakota told her.

Emily laughed. "I can make sandwiches. Will that work?"

"Just sandwiches?" Cooper asked.

"Sandwiches are enough, Coop. Christ." Storm grinned up at Emily.

She started to say something but saw another truck pull up. Nathan and his fiancée stepped out and walked toward the porch.

"This is my fiancée, Shelly Tillman. Shell, this is Emily and Lucas Taggart."

Shelly was a petite blonde with green eyes, and beautiful. She looked to be in her early thirties. "It's nice to meet you both." She smiled shyly at Emily and Lucas.

"Why is someone as beautiful as you engaged to this ugly guy?" Lucas laughed.

Dakota put his arm around Shelly's shoulders. "I told her she was marrying the wrong brother."

Nathan lifted Dakota's arm from Shelly's shoulders. "Back off. You know I can kick your ass."

Shelly stepped away from both of them rolling her eyes. "We can talk inside, Emily. This macho BS is too much to deal with."

The men laughed and headed for the truck to unload everything. Nathan followed the women inside and headed for his deputy who was taking pictures. Shelly sighed.

"He can't even relax for a minute."

Emily smiled. "He's a cop. It's what he does."

"I know but just once I wish he'd slow down." Shelly stared in the direction Nathan had gone.

Emily gazed at her and smiled. Shelly loved Nathan very much. Emily could see it on Shelly's face. When Shelly turned to face her, Emily's smile grew.

"What?" Shelly asked, narrowing her eyes.

"You are so in love with that man." Emily chuckled.

Shelly burst out laughing. "Yes, I am. Does it show that much?"

Emily was about to answer when Nathan came back into the kitchen with his deputy following him. He came to a halt, looked at each woman, and then raised an eyebrow at Shelly. She grinned at him.

"Why do I get the feeling you were talking about me?" Nathan muttered.

The women laughed. "Maybe we were." Shelly said as she moved closer to him and wrapped her arms around his waist.

Nathan put his arms around her and hugged her. "Emily, you can clean up."

Emily made a face. "If I must."

"I'll help you. Let's do it then we'll make the men some sandwiches." Shelly stood on tiptoe and kissed Nathan's lips. He grinned and walked out the door, his deputy following.

Emily got the cleaning supplies and the women cleaned the blood in the hallway and swept up the shattered glass through the house. When they finished, they prepared sandwiches and drinks for the men. Shelly walked out onto the porch to tell them to come in and eat. They each washed their hands and sat at the table. Nathan pulled Shelly onto his lap.

"None of that at the table, big brother," Dakota said as he reached for a sandwich.

"You're just jealous you don't have someone." Nathan teased him.

Dakota winked at Shelly. "Are you sure you don't want to run away with me?"

Shelly laughed. "No, I think I'll keep this one."

"You *think* you will?" Nathan growled making everyone laugh.

Emily glanced over to see Lucas looking at her. She raised her eyebrows at him. He grinned and mouthed 'later' to her making her blush. After the men ate, they sauntered back outside. Emily couldn't keep the smile from her face as she watched Lucas walk across the yard to the truck, back to work. She turned to see Shelly smiling at her.

"You love that man a lot." Shelly laughed.

Emily blushed but nodded and laughed with her new friend. "So tell me how you and Nathan met."

Shelly smiled. "I was on a date with Dakota." At Emily's gasp, Shelly went on. "It was our first and last date. We were out for dinner and ran into Nathan and Carol Dunbar. As soon as Nathan and I looked at each other, I knew he was the one. He said he thought the same thing." Shelly shrugged. "Thing is, Carol saw it too. Nathan asked us to sit with them. At first Dakota didn't want to but Carol talked him into it. Nathan and I couldn't keep our eyes off each other. When I went to the restroom, Carol did too. I thought for sure she was going to jump all over me for staring at her date." Shelly laughed. "Boy, did she fool me. She said she could feel the 'pull' between us. I didn't know what to say. When we returned to the table, she asked Dakota to take her home. He looked at her like she was crazy but it dawned on him what was going on. He smiled, took her hand and they left together. Nathan sat there staring at me and I thought maybe I was wrong, then he smiled and we've been together ever since."

"Fantastic story. When's the wedding?"

"Christmas Eve day. I want a winter wedding. I want to be a snow bride." Shelly laughed. "Nathan thinks I'm crazy but I love snow and I've always dreamed of a wedding in winter. He picked the day."

"I was a winter bride but I didn't get to plan too far ahead." Emily shook her head.

"I know. Nathan told me about it, but you and Lucas love each other now and that's all that matters. If Nathan wanted to elope, I'd do it in a heartbeat. I adore the man."

"I'm sure the feeling is mutual. I noticed he can't keep his eyes or hands off you."

Shelly blushed prettily. "I hope you and Lucas will come to the wedding. It's not going to be a large affair. Just family and some close friends. I'd love it if you two would come."

Emily nodded. "We'd love to," she said as Lucas walked in the backdoor.

"We'd love to what?" he asked.

"Attend Nathan and Shelly's wedding."

Lucas grinned at Shelly. "Sure. I want to see Nathan get married. He's avoided it for years." Lucas winked at her. "Just took the right woman." He glanced at Emily. "That's all it ever takes."

The men came in the back door loud and boisterous. Playfully shoving each other around until Nathan came in behind them, telling them to quiet down. "They're like a bunch of kids." He shook his head.

"Get used to it, big brother, if you want kids one day." Dakota teased.

"They still wouldn't be as childish as you."

Emily laughed along with everyone else. She wanted to start a family soon and hoped Lucas did too. The thought of a little boy running after his daddy as he worked on the ranch and learned how to ride a horse made her smile. Her grandfather had her on a horse when she was in diapers and she wanted the same for her children.

She wanted to watch Lucas ride with their child in front of him on the saddle. She wanted to see their children grow up loving horses as much as she and Lucas did.

Emily snapped out of her daydream as everyone started to leave. Shelly hugged her. "I've enjoyed meeting you and our talk. It was nice. Let's get together soon."

Emily hugged her back. "I'd love to. We'll get together for lunch one day next week."

Shelly smiled at her as Nathan took her hand in his and led her out the door. Lucas stood on the porch as his friends pulled out. He entered the kitchen and strode to her. Cupping her face in his hands, he kissed her.

"I missed you today," he murmured against her lips.

Emily grinned. "I've been right here."

Lucas snorted. "I know, but I couldn't get away to come see you."

"You were busy and you all got a lot accomplished today."

"We only need to finish the kitchen and back of the house and it'll be as good as new." Lucas started to lead her from the kitchen. "I need a shower."

"So why are you taking me with you? I don't need one." She squealed when he picked her up and tossed her over his shoulder.

"You need to learn what I say goes," Lucas growled.

Emily burst out laughing. "Yeah, sure."

Lucas smacked her bottom. "Smart ass." He trudged up the stairs and into their bedroom and moved toward the bed. He laid her down on it then leaned over her and kissed her. Emily opened to him and wrapped her arms around his neck as he deepened the kiss. His tongue moved into her mouth and he groaned when she touched hers to his.

"God, I want you so much Emily," he told her as he moved his lips across her cheek to her ear. He sucked her earlobe into his mouth and sucked on it. She shivered and felt him grin. His lips moved down her neck as he unbuttoned her blouse and swept it open then he opened the front clasp on her bra, letting her breasts spill free. Lucas moved his mouth down her chest to take a nipple into his mouth. He sucked deeply. Emily's fingers plowed through his hair and pulled him closer. She arched her back and groaned as he moved to the other nipple.

His hand moved down to the snap of her jeans and unhooked it then his hand moved under her panties to the wet folds of her femininity. Moving the pad of his thumb against her clitoris, he inserted two fingers. Lucas moved them in and out as his thumb moved against her. Emily's legs tightened against his hand and her muscles clenched around him when she came and cried out his name.

He stood and shucked his clothes then knelt beside her and rolled her to her stomach. He moved behind her, lifted her to her knees, and thrust into her hard and fast. Emily screamed out as Lucas pounded into her. She arched back toward him. His hands moved to her hips to set a rhythm. Emily was going over the edge again.

"Lucas…" She groaned as another orgasm hit her. A low moan came from deep in his chest as he followed her over. Her knees gave out and she fell forward with Lucas on top of her. He rolled off her.

"Are you all right?" he whispered.

"Yes. You?" She started to giggle.

"Yes. What's funny?"

"I thought we came up here to shower?"

"Did I say that? I said I needed a shower. Now you do too."

Emily smiled at him. "I'll wash yours if you wash mine."

Lucas laughed. "Deal." He stood and put his hand out to her. She placed her hand in his and they headed for the bathroom. "Then we'll take a nap. I need one."

Emily nodded. "Sounds good to me."

They slept until the next morning.

* * * *

The last week of June was a scorcher. Emily sat on the front porch watching the slight breeze move the dust around the driveway. She needed to go inside but her thoughts were on Lucas. He seemed distant over the past week and she wasn't sure why. He barely spoke. He'd just come in from working, shower, eat, and go to bed. It scared her. The only conversations they seemed to have revolved around business.

Emily stood and walked into the house. There was paperwork to do and it would take her mind off things. Things being Lucas. As she sat at the desk, she couldn't get past the thought he wasn't happy any longer. But why? They hadn't made love in a week. Granted, it was the breeding season for the horses and sales were up but that couldn't be it, could it? She sighed and pulled out the ledger. Looking at the numbers usually made her smile but not today. Today she hurt because she was terrified she was losing him. Since Adam was dead, there really was no reason for Lucas to stick around.

Tossing down the pen, she strode from the room, through the kitchen and out the back door. She was going to get to the bottom of this now. When she entered the barn, she allowed her eyes to adjust before heading down the aisle. She heard voices coming from one of the stalls and headed toward it. Emily recognized Tinker's and Lucas's voices but she came to a dead stop when she heard what Lucas was saying.

"I can't help it, Tinker. I'm restless."

"You need to get over it. You ain't been married but a few months for Christ's sake. Give it time," Tinker raised his voice.

"I tried. I can't anymore. It's like an itch I can't scratch."

"You have time. You're young yet. Both of you."

"That's exactly why I want it now," Lucas argued.

Emily couldn't stand to hear anymore, she turned and ran from the barn. Once inside the house, she ran upstairs, threw herself across the bed, and let the tears go. He wanted to leave her. He was restless again and wanted to leave like he left Wyoming five years ago. After a few minutes, she sat up and glanced around the room they shared. He wasn't going to do this to her. She'd end it first before he had a chance to.

Emily got up and pulled his clothes out of the closet and tossed them in his duffle bag then dragged it down the stairs and set it by the front door. Then she sat in the living room and waited for him to come in the back door.

* * * *

Lucas entered the kitchen and called for Emily. When she didn't answer, he headed toward the living room and found her sitting in the window seat staring out the window.

"Didn't you hear me calling for you?" Lucas smiled at her. When she didn't smile back, he frowned at her. He glanced around not knowing what to say. His duffle bag sat by the front door. "Why's my duffle bag there?" He had a sick feeling.

"I packed it for you. I want you to leave." She stood to face him.

"Leave? Why?"

Emily shrugged. "Adam's dead. I don't need you anymore."

"I own half this ranch." Lucas's temper was rising.

"Whenever you get where you're going, let me know and I'll send you a check every month."

Lucas clenched his jaw and his fists. "You'll send me..." He couldn't go on without shouting and he didn't want to do that.

"You're not needed here anymore, Lucas. In fact, I killed Adam. You were right when you said you didn't protect me very well."

His heart slammed into his ribs and he swallowed hard. "So you don't need me at all now."

"Apparently, I never did. Please go." She turned away from him.

Lucas stared at her for a few seconds then gave a terse nod. "Fine." He picked up his duffle bag and headed out. He softly closed the door when he wanted to slam it so hard the glass would break. What the hell happened? She said she loved him. Lucas tossed his duffle bag into the bed of the truck and got in. His knuckles turned white as he gripped the steering wheel. His gaze roamed over the barns and horses in the corrals. He loved Whispering Pines but he loved Emily more. He'd give everything he owned to have her in his life. He didn't give a rat's ass about the ranch, he only wanted her. Taking a deep breath, he started the truck and with one more glance at the house, he turned the truck around and pulled out, spinning tires and throwing gravel. With no destination in mind, he drove toward Lincoln's ranch. Lucas could stay there with him. He knew Linc would take him in, no questions asked. Lucas shook his head as he drove toward Linc's place. They'd wanted a family. *What the hell happened?* He slammed his fist against the steering wheel. There would never be another woman for him. Emily was his life and now he was supposed to go on without her. Lucas shook his head. He just didn't understand what happened.

* * * *

When Emily heard the door click shut behind him, she collapsed to the floor. How she held up when she wanted to beg him not to leave her was a miracle. Tears rolled down her cheeks as she listened to him walk across the porch and then his truck starting up and him driving off. Why was he the kind of man who got restless? She thought he loved Whispering Pines. She thought he loved her. He'd said it over and over but he wanted to go. Why was he unhappy when he owned half of the best Quarter Horse ranch in the states? The thought of going on without him was a pain like no other.

Munch butted her head against her and meowed. Emily sat up and stared at her. "I ran him off, Munch." She pulled the cat onto her lap. "He got restless and I made him go before he had to tell me. I don't know what I'm going to do without him." Sobs shook her body as she held the cat to her. Munch pushed at her and Emily let her go. "You don't want me either."

Emily stood and walked upstairs. She bypassed the bedroom she'd shared with Lucas. There was no way she could sleep in the bed she'd once shared with him. Going into her room, she laid on the bed and stared at the ceiling. Why was she so bad at picking men? Adam had been a criminal and Lucas had been...wonderful. Rolling to her side, she hugged her pillow and cried. They'd talked about having a family. She wanted his children so badly and now it would never happen. Lucas had enough money to buy his own place or travel and it seemed like he wanted to travel. He was out of her life. There was paperwork she needed to do, but it could wait. She'd catch up with it tomorrow and try to get on with her life.

* * * *

Lucas woke up the next morning after only a few hours sleep. He'd tossed and turned all night trying to figure out what went wrong. Reaching out for her and not finding her. *Christ!* He sat up and swung his legs over the side of the bed ad rubbed his temples. He had one hell of a headache. He stood, stretched, and then headed for the shower. Linc hadn't asked a thing and Lucas knew he'd wait for Lucas to say something first. That's how Lincoln was. Laid back and patient.

Lucas walked downstairs and entered the kitchen. He got himself a cup of coffee and took a seat at the table. Lincoln came in the back door.

"Son of a bitch, it's hot out already," He told Lucas as he strode to the refrigerator and grabbed a bottle of water. He drank half of it before he sat down across from Lucas. "Do you want to help me in the barn today or are you moving on?"

"I'll help out. I don't know what I'm going to do yet."

Lincoln nodded. "You can stay here as long as you need."

"I appreciate it, Linc." Lucas huffed. "She told me to leave. Said she didn't need me anymore since Walters is dead and I didn't do a good job of protecting her anyway since she's the one who killed him."

"It doesn't sound right to me. Are you sure you didn't piss her off in some way?"

"No. I've been busy with all the breeding and sales going on but we talked every night before we'd go to bed."

Lincoln shook his head. "You're crazy about her."

Lucas smirked. "I love her more than life."

"Did you tell her?"

Lucas nodded. "Yes and she said she loved me too. I just don't get it." He sighed. "I thought we were happy. We talked about having kids."

Lincoln tossed the empty water bottle into the bin. "I'll be in the barn when you feel like coming out. I've got a stallion who hates everyone and everything."

Lucas nodded. Lincoln had a reputation for being the best 'horse whisperer' in the state of Wyoming. People brought their horses from near and far to get him to work with their horses. People said he could take the wildest stallion from the plains and have it eating out of his hand in no time. Lucas believed it since he'd been a witness to Lincoln's work with horses. It always amazed him.

Sighing, he stood and headed for the barn. He'd shuck stalls if he had to. Anything to try to keep his mind off Emily.

* * * *

Emily entered the barn to let Tinker know Lucas was gone. He came strolling toward her and smiled. "Good morning, Emily." He stopped and stared at her. "You look tired. Didn't you sleep? And where's Lucas?"

"I didn't sleep well." Emily cleared her throat. "Uh...Lucas is gone."

"Gone? Where? We didn't have a feed pick up scheduled. Did he go to town?"

"No. He's...gone. He left. It's over between us." Her voice caught on a sob.

Tinker reared back. "What do you mean, over?"

"He's gone, all right? Just let it go, Tinker, and get the men started on their chores. I don't want to talk about it. No," she said when he started to interrupt. "The subject is closed. I'll be in the back office. I don't want to be disturbed." She strode past him and headed to the office. She could hear Tinker muttering behind her but she ignored him.

As she sat at the desk, she noticed the clock she'd given Lucas to remind him of the time. He always let it slip away when he sat at the desk to enter the day's activities. She'd teased him he'd come in at midnight if he didn't have the clock. He'd teased back, saying he'd still wake her up if he did.

Emily placed her hands over her face as she felt the tears welling up in her eyes again. There shouldn't be any tears left since she'd cried all night. Four hours of sleep was going to wear her down through the day but for now, she had to get to work. Maybe she'd take a nap later. She snorted. She knew that wouldn't happen. With Lucas gone, she'd pick up the slack, doing what she'd done before he came to the ranch.

Emily jumped when someone knocked at the office door. Sighing, she told them to come in and groaned when she saw Tinker. She should have known he wouldn't let it go.

"It's none of your business, Tinker."

"I just wanted to know if you still had plans to breed Cinnamon with Blue, since Blue belongs to Lucas."

She shook her head. "I don't know."

"Lucas wanted them to have a foal together but if he tore out of here, what he wants don't much matter. I think you should sell his horse anyway. We don't need him here anymore than we need Lucas here." He practically marched from the office.

Emily knew he was hurting too. Tinker loved Lucas and he was upset Lucas was gone. She sat back in the chair and stared out the window. Even though Tinker shouldn't be surprised Lucas was gone since she'd heard Tinker trying to talk him out of it. Tinker probably thought he'd convinced Lucas to stay and was angry he hadn't been able to talk him into it. They'd get through this. They had to. Whispering Pines would go on without the other owner. Once Lucas let her know where he was, she'd mail him his checks. Even that was going to be hard on her. Writing his name on a check and envelope. She wasn't looking forward to it at all.

* * * *

Two weeks later, it seemed as if she worried for nothing. Lucas hadn't contacted her at all. Where was he? Did he miss her at all? Like she missed him? Emily hadn't slept at all and it was catching up to her. She dragged her feet out to the barn in the mornings and practically crawled to the house at night. Tinker kept an eye on her but didn't say anything until the day she almost passed out. He caught her before she hit the floor.

"I'm all right, Tinker."

"The hell you are," He roared. "You're not sleeping or eating and you're killing yourself out here. I don't know what happened between you and Lucas but it's obvious you're falling apart without him."

Emily jerked away from him. "Don't you tell me you don't know what happened. I heard you. I heard you both," she shouted.

Tinker frowned. "Heard us? Heard us about what?"

"He said he was restless and you tried to tell him to give it time. I told him to go so I wouldn't have to hear him tell me he was leaving me."

"Wait. You *told* him to leave?" At her nod, he took his hat off and threw it to the floor. "I can't believe you. You know I love you, you're like a daughter to me, but if you'd have just come in and asked what we were talking about instead of jumping to conclusions, Lucas would still be here," his voice rose as he ranted.

"What are you saying, Tinker?" Emily whispered.

"Damn woman! He was talking about wanting children. He was getting restless thinking about them but he wasn't sure you were ready. I told him since you hadn't been married long to give it time. You were both young."

Emily put her hand over her mouth and shook her head. "No."

"Yes. Now he's gone and we're all miserable, especially you." Tinker picked his hat up. "I don't know how, but you need to find him. I'm sure you broke his heart. That man loves you more than anything. I know that, even if you don't." He strode away from her.

The tears in her eyes overflowed and rolled down her cheeks. How could she have been so stupid? Why had she doubted him? He loved her. Lucas wasn't the type of man to say it if he didn't mean it. He didn't need to say it to get anything from her, he already owned half the ranch. He had more than enough money of his own, he didn't need hers. When he told her he loved her, he meant it and she made him leave. She groaned. The things she'd said to him were unforgivable. He had protected her from Adam. He kept her safe and she'd told him he hadn't. What kind of wife says those kind of things to her husband? She could see the look on his face as if he stood in front of her now. The hurt was plain to see but she hadn't seen it then. The hurt blinded her as it surely did him. Emily picked up her cell phone and called his friends. They all said they had no idea where he was, until she called Mont.

"Agent Bradford," he answered.

"Mont..." She cleared her throat. "This is Emily...Taggart. Do you know where Lucas is?"

"Don't you?" Came his snappish response.

Emily winced. "No. I was hoping you did. He...left here two--"

"He left or you told him to leave?"

"I told him to leave but it was a misunderstanding."

"I always thought married couples worked things out instead of giving up."

"Mont, please. I need to find him," Emily pleaded.

"I'll see what I can do." He disconnected the call.

Emily stared at her phone, not believing he'd hung up on her. She was positive all of Lucas's friends knew where he was, they just weren't going to tell her. Apparently, Lucas had told them what happened.

Later in the evening, she saw truck lights coming up the driveway and her heart hit her stomach when she recognized Lucas's truck. He was home! She ran toward the kitchen and waited for him to enter the house. She planned to throw herself at him. A few minutes went by and he still hadn't come in. Emily moved toward the door and peered out. His truck sat at the entrance to the barn, a horse trailer on the back. He was there to pick up Blue, not to see her. Well, if he thought it was going to be easy, he was in for a shock. Emily ran out to the barn and moved around his truck to stand at the back of the trailer.

* * * *

Lucas led Blue from the stall and stopped in his tracks when he saw Emily standing by the trailer. He took a deep breath and moved forward. Lord, it hurt to look at her. The closer he got to her the more he wanted to pull her into his arms and never let her go, but she didn't want him or his horse. He shook his head.

"If you would have just told me the day you made me leave to take my horse, I wouldn't have had to come back."

Emily frowned at him. "What?"

Lucas huffed. "I didn't think you'd want me to take Blue or I would have."

She shook her head. "What are you talking about?"

Lucas clenched his jaw. "Mont told me you called him and said to tell me to come get Blue." He shrugged. "I would have taken him when you first told me to leave if you'd have let me know."

"Mont told..." Emily laughed then slapped her hand over her mouth.

Lucas narrowed his eyes at her. "Is that funny?"

Emily nodded. "Yes, since I didn't tell Mont any such thing."

"What?" Lucas scowled at her. "Of course you did. Mont wouldn't lie…" Lucas swore. "If this is his idea of a joke, he's a dead man."

"I did call him but to see if he knew where you were."

"Of course he knew. I was staying with him. I think I found some property in Butte I might buy."

"You can't buy it."

"Why the hell not?"

"You own land here," she said softly.

"I'll sell it back to you. I don't want it." He led Blue into the trailer. When he came back out and started to close the door, she stood in his way.

"I don't want your half, Lucas." She gazed up at him. "I just want you."

"You told me to leave."

"I heard you tell Tinker you were restless. I thought you meant you needed to take off. I sent you away before you had a chance to leave me."

"I was talking about children." He shook his head.

"I know that now. Tinker told me. It's why I wanted to find you. To apologize and ask you to forgive me and come home." A tear rolled down her cheek.

Lucas reached out and caught it then he pulled her into his arms. "I never want to go anywhere you aren't, Emily. I love you. I want to have children and then I'll have everything I could ever want in this life." He gazed down into her face and lowered his lips to hers. Her arms circled around his neck and her legs around his waist when he lifted her up.

"I'm so sorry for jumping to conclusions." She rained kisses over his face.

"You should have asked me what I was talking about," he growled.

"I will from now on. I promise not to jump to conclusions. I love you, Lucas."

They jumped when a throat cleared behind them. They turned to see Tinker smiling at them.

"I sure am glad to see you home, boss."

Lucas laughed. "I'm glad to see you and be home too, Tinker. Now, if you wouldn't mind, could you take Blue out of the trailer for me? My wife and I have some catching up to do." He chuckled when Emily blushed. "And we'll work on those kids," he whispered.

Epilogue
Christmas Eve Day

"You look so beautiful, Shelly," Emily said as she fixed Shelly's veil.

"I'm so nervous. What if he doesn't show up?"

Emily laughed. "Oh, please. Nathan will be here. He loves you." She knew it was just nerves talking. Shelly didn't doubt Nathan's love. Emily strolled to the door when a knock sounded. She opened it to Shelly's sister, Kathy, who was her maid of honor.

"Hi Emily. Is she still nervous about him not showing up?" Kathy smiled. The sisters were both blonde and beautiful but where Shelly was petite, Kathy was statuesque.

"Yes. I told her not to worry, he'd be here."

Kathy moved to her sister. "You look so beautiful. He's here. I just saw him so now you can smile." Kathy laughed when Shelly beamed.

"I'll just slip out and leave you two alone." Emily smiled. She knew the sisters wanted time alone.

"Emily," Shelly's voice stopped her. She turned to look at her. "Thank you for being a friend. I'm so glad we met over the summer. You've been a tremendous help to me."

Emily grinned. "My pleasure. I'm so happy you're marrying Nathan and I hope you'll be as happy as Lucas and I are." She softly closed the door and headed for the church. She spotted Lucas standing in the vestibule, talking on his cell phone. He stuck it in his pocket and frowned.

"Are you all right, Lucas?"

"Mont said he's going off the grid for a while. I won't be able to contact him at all."

"Does he do that often?"

"First time I've heard of it." Lucas shook his head. "He said he'll call me when he gets back. I don't like it."

Emily kissed his cheek. "He's FBI. He knows what he's doing."

Lucas ran his eyes over her. "You look beautiful in your green dress, Missus Taggart."

Emily glanced down at the skintight green dress. "I won't be able to get in to it much longer."

"Are you telling me you're gaining weight, darlin'?" Lucas chuckled.

"That's exactly what I'm saying, Mister Taggart." She kept her gaze fixed on his face.

Lucas frowned then his eyes widened as dawning set in. "Pregnant?"

"Yep." Emily almost squealed when he grasped her hand and led her down a hallway. He put her back against a wall.

"You couldn't have told me this earlier?" he growled.

Emily laughed. "No. I know you. We wouldn't have made it to the wedding and I had to help Shelly with her gown."

Lucas buried his face in her neck. "You'll pay for that."

"I can't wait."

"Let's go sit down. We won't ruin their day by telling anyone until tomorrow, but tonight, you and I are celebrating. I love you, Emily Taggart."

"I love you, Lucas Taggart."

Lucas kissed her quickly and led her into the church pew. They sat and waited for the ceremony to start. Emily leaned over toward him.

"Did I tell you twins run in my family?" She laughed when Lucas groaned.

The End

About the Author

Susan was born and raised in Cumberland, MD. She moved to Tennessee in 1996 with her husband. She now lives in a small town outside of Nashville, along with her husband and their two rescued dogs. Susan is a huge Nashville Predators hockey fan. She also enjoys fishing, taking drives down back roads, and visiting Gatlinburg, TN. She would love to hear from her readers and promises to try to respond to all. You can visit her Facebook page and website by the links below.
https://www.facebook.com/skdromanceauthor
www.susanfisherdavisauthor.weebly.com

Other books by Susan Fisher-Davis

Jake (Men of Clifton Montana Book 1)
Gabe (Men of Clifton Montana Book 2)

CPSIA information can be obtained
at www.ICGtesting.com
Printed in the USA
LVOW13s0216130917
548519LV00022B/832/P